D0908841

SMELL THE RAIN-DROPS

SMELL THE RAINDROPS

BA AUSTIN

Crescendo
PRESS

© 2015 by B.A. Austin. All rights reserved.

Crescendo Press
165 13th Street
Del Mar, California 92014
crescendo-press.com

Edited by Graciela Sholander
Front cover design by Mike C Green at blatantcreative.com
Interior design by Charles McStravick

Cataloging-in-Publication Data is on file at the Library of Congress

Tradepaper ISBN: 978-0-9895047-3-7
ePub ISBN: 978-0-9895047-5-1

10 9 8 7 6 5 4 3 2 1

PRINTED IN THE UNITED STATES OF AMERICA

In memory of Karine,
whom I am truly blessed to have known.

Dedicated to my children:
I love you so dearly.
Without you, I may not have been here
to write my story.

CONTENTS

IF MY CONSCIENCE
HAS A FACE

As I watch the glowing orb of the sun dip below the horizon line of the infinite Pacific Ocean, thoughts race through my mind like the waves that crash intermittently along the shore below me, sometimes with force, other times with a calm and startling peace, not one ripple to be found. Sitting on a park bench upon these Southern California cliffs, gazing at the vastness before me, I feel transported to a place where time and space have no boundaries, no definition. While golden rays reflect off the shimmering water, I find myself reflecting on the life I've led these past six decades.

It's funny how after all these years the Pacific Ocean and that mighty, muddy Mississippi River from my past can become one, the passage of time seemingly inexistent. I walk through long corridors of my mind, trying to remember everything. Trying to gather the pieces, retrace steps, discover the meaning behind each moment. Reaching into the past, I see shades, hints, and whispers of the person I am today, the mother and grandmother I have become. I don't feel that far removed from the little Southern girl I once was. Always beside me, first in person and now in spirit I feel profoundly, is the steady, gentle presence of Karine.

My dear Karine, what would my life have been without you? I dare not imagine. Growing up in Memphis, Tennessee, I was raised by three people: Mom, Dad, and Karine. Though my childhood was a privileged one by many standards, lived in comfort and relative ease, it was Karine, the lovely black woman who cared for me as if I'd emerged from her own womb, who gave me strength to overcome challenges that loomed like storm clouds over the horizon. She was my rock, my spiritual teacher, my refuge. From my innocent childhood days along the mighty Mississippi River, to my college years by the stormy Atlantic, and on to my life as a grown woman by the endless blue Pacific, I have been nurtured and sustained by her love.

Even though she's long gone from this world, Karine is the one person who has remained with me to guide my steps. How could I ever forget her? She is a vital part of my very being. Our hearts, though broken open time and again, are forever intertwined.

If my conscience has a face, it's the tender, smiling countenance of Karine. When I doubt myself, she is the one who whispers, "I have faith in you, child." When I am about to set off on a path to self-destruction, she is there, trying to gently nudge me in a better direction. I can feel her selflessly guiding me at every juncture of my life, her spirit somehow seeing me through great joys and personal lows, always lifting me back up when I need redemption.

But I'm getting ahead of myself. As I rest here on this park bench on the cliffs high above the Pacific, let me try to piece it all together from the beginning, from the days when I was a little tomboy with soft strawberry blonde curls blowing in the fresh Southern breeze ...

CHAPTER ONE

AT THE PEARLY GATES
OF HEAVEN

People think of the land of Dixie as hot and humid, but that's only half the story. Believe me, Memphis has seasons and winters can get mighty cold. I remember that particularly wet and dreary day in the winter of 1959. Through a misty filter I can still picture my reflection in the mirror—my soft round face, hazel eyes, freckled nose, chubby legs. These were the features of the sweet, carefree innocence of the five-year-old I was. More vividly, I remember the moment Karine walked into my life. She arrived at my family's kitchen door for her first day of work and, as she stepped inside, the room lit up with her maternal warmth.

My family and I had recently moved out of our family oriented, middle-class neighborhood on a cul-de-sac where the streets were busy with kids looking to play with one another. Those early years of my life were filled with games of hide-and-seek and kickball, trick-or-treating, and building snowmen, and every Sunday my family and I walked to our Presbyterian church. I so clearly remember the day we left; I sat in the back of our Chevy wagon, staring out the window and waving goodbye to all the kids and moms and dads as they stood lined up along the sidewalks. Four-year-old Susie, my best girlfriend, was there, with the cutest dimples and long brown curls, sadly waving goodbye.

We moved into quite a unique, award-winning home out in the country on a quiet road. Sleek, modern, and spacious, our house was tucked away in acres of beautiful woods. In Memphis it was the norm for white children like my brothers and me to be taken care of by black ladies like Karine. My parents were well-off and could afford to hire household help. That day when she walked into our lives, Karine stood in our kitchen wearing her long, tattered wool coat, worn-out black boots, and a black wool hat. Underneath her hat was the kindest smile I had ever seen. She was in her early sixties, with both motherly and grandmotherly nuances about her, but she possessed a glow and energy usually found in someone much younger.

Shyly, I peered up at her. Her warm eyes gently focused on mine.

"Nice to meet you, Miss Bethany Ann. My name is Karine."

I bit my lip and simply kept watching her, too bashful to speak. Without saying a word, she swooped me up and sat me on the kitchen counter. Leaning over, she looked straight into my eyes and proceeded to tell me about the pearly gates of Heaven. I was mesmerized. I sat still, enraptured by the sweet, lulling sound of her confident voice, listening closely to every word. As Karine shared with me wondrous tales of Heaven, something special happened. An uncommon friendship formed, a friendship that kept me going through my childhood and teen years and continues to fortify me to this day.

Though I was born Bethany Ann, Mom thought I should be called simply Ann in school. I don't know why. Maybe Bethany Ann sounded too small-town for a student of the prep school for proper young ladies I attended. Only my family called me Bethany Ann. Or sometimes, for short, they called me Bannie.

We were a typical family of five, although in many ways we weren't typical at all, certainly not for the times. My father, Ted, was a hardworking man. Barely 30, Dad already knew the meaning of success. He ran prominent car dealerships in Memphis and Beverly Hills, California. This was the business to be in; Americans had a love affair with the automobile, dreaming of the wide, open spaces they could roam across in their shiny cars. The Chevy symbolized freedom in every sense of the word. Dad capitalized on this craze, doing well financially for himself and our family.

Like all good businessmen, though, he paid a price. He worked tirelessly 24/7. In his office he was set up with a Murphy bed—a bed that pops out of the wall and, when not in use, conveniently hides vertically in a cabinet—and a shower for the many long, taxing workdays he spent away from home. Business was very good, but it certainly wasn't easy. In 1952 he was quoted in a local newspaper as saying, "This business is a time-consuming proposition ... there's always something to do ... there is no such thing as getting everything done, because you've got to keep thinking ahead." Strict dedication to his career and a keen business sense made Dad a successful man.

Dad loved running his dealership in Southern California, but I'm quite certain that moving the family was never an option. My mother Jo Ann knew with all her heart that Memphis was the right place for us. She saw Los Angeles as a shallow, empty sort of place obsessed with the image it strove to create, a poor choice for raising her family. Mom wasn't impressed with movie stars, famous Hollywood Boulevard, palm trees lined up in neat rows, the Beach Boys, or the buzz you could find on practically every street corner. No, that was not the place for us. We were Southerners, and Memphis had everything we needed—family, strong Christian values, and creek-filled woods far away from glitz.

This is not to say that I didn't feel the allure of Hollywood now and then. Even though we lived almost 2,000 miles away, we had a few traces of Tinseltown scattered throughout the house. My favorite was a framed black and white photo of Mom and Dad standing with a voluptuous blonde actress named Jayne Mansfield who was every bit as captivating as Marilyn Monroe. Each time I walked past that picture my eyes would linger and, for a moment, I'd get lost in a reverie of glamour, of a place that was worlds away from the one I knew.

My world was a child's paradise. Matt—one of my two big brothers—and I took full advantage of the wooded ten acres surrounding our home. Together with our faithful German Shepherd, Scout—best friend a child could have—we romped all over stretches of verdant woods filled with vines and creeks and numerous species of animals that only a child would be unafraid or unaware of. We'd leave the world behind, creating a new one in its wake, succumbing to the mystical rhythms of nature. We were explorers, adventurers.

One of our favorite games was playing Tarzan in our imaginary jungle. Matt, who was almost two years older but more like my inseparable twin than a big brother, played Tarzan while I was always Cheeta, his chimp friend (I never minded). We would swing on sturdy vines across cool, rippling creeks for hours on end. Then we'd crawl through several miles of dark sewer drains, never having a clue as to what dead rat or other varmint we could stumble over. Not knowing was part of the fun. There was nothing for me to fear, because Matt was Tarzan, my big brother, my best friend, my protector. Everywhere he went he had a mischievous twinkle in his eye. He was energetic, fun, and full of insatiable curiosity.

Will was the oldest of the three of us. Nearly four years older than me, he was in many ways more of a father figure than a big brother. Stoic, quiet, and responsible, he liked to keep to himself. He didn't join Matt and me in our backyard adventures. Instead, he dove into books, one right after another. Will loved to shut himself up in his bedroom to read for hours. Fun for him was reading the encyclopedia from A to Z. And doing the daily crossword puzzle.

Our picture-perfect house was home for thirteen years. Strikingly unique for the traditional South in the late fifties and early sixties, it was a dramatic 10,000-square-foot Japanese style house with naturally aged cedar and enormous floor to ceiling windows offering a panoramic view of the swimming pool and wooded grounds. Spacious rooms, high ceilings, and dramatic angles caused guests to take pause and stare with reverence and disbelief. Our atrium contained an authentic Japanese garden. Walls throughout the house were decorated with intricate 800-year-old Japanese screens. Ancient Japanese artifacts were arranged carefully in each room, enhancing every nook and cranny. Sliding cherry wood panels were held by beams instead of walls, adding to our home's openness and roominess. There was no shortage of style here.

The outdoor gardens were equally enchanting, spreading over rolling hills through wooded grounds filled with a cornucopia of intoxicating scents and sounds. I was swept up by it all: The aroma of freshly mown grass, the rumbling of thunder in the distance, gentle raindrops, the melodic sounds of the whippoorwill and bobwhite. Not to mention the palette of colors we enjoyed—red tulips, yellow daffodils, lavender hyacinths, white dogwood blossoms. Our property was something straight out of *Architectural Digest*.

The daily morning newspaper in Memphis ran a piece about our house in the fall of 1965, describing it as "... a perfect Japanese house in a Memphis setting." Indeed, our home sat in perfect accord with the natural beauty of the land. One year it served as the setting for the annual Ikebana festival, celebrating the age-old art of Japanese flower arranging. In 1960, our home won the first honor award of the American Institute of Architecture. Another year it was chosen by the Architectural Record among "Record Selections."

My parents, my brothers, and I blended into our surroundings almost as well as the house blended into its picturesque environment. Mom was something of a Jacqueline Kennedy with her impeccable style of dress, from her chic sunglasses to her Chanel outfits. She was the model wife of a young, successful businessman, full of grace, charm, and sincerity. Mom was also an extremely generous, giving woman. She never passed up the opportunity to immerse herself in volunteer work. She spent hours upon hours pouring her energy into an organization that served children with severe handicaps. Both my parents were very private, and country club parties did not appeal to Mom. She preferred a quiet afternoon of lunch and shopping with a few of her closest friends.

Most of the credit for our home's beauty went to Keith and Howard, my parents' interior designers. For them, traveling to New York City and San Francisco to buy Oriental furniture and rare objects was a regular occurrence. They lived for beauty, and they enjoyed the free rein Mom and Dad gave them to turn our house into a Japanese jewel. I thought of Keith and Howard as kindly, creative uncles, and I always enjoyed their visits. Throughout my life they traveled the world with us, from the Caribbean to the Mediterranean.

Our home would not have been complete without Karine, AJ, and Elsa, the black folk who worked for us. We regarded them as family and, in turn, we were the only family Karine and AJ had. Will, Matt, and I were lovingly raised by Karine, and AJ graciously chauffeured us around town.

Karine, ever my conscience, was the first person I turned to whenever I had a question about life. I loved Keith and Howard dearly, but their tight-knit relationship befuddled me. Without thinking twice, I approached Karine one day, curious to know more about our interior designer friends, and asked, "Keith and Howard ... why do they live together?"

Karine answered simply, "Honey, they love one another and are two very fine men. Don't let anyone tell you different."

And that was that. Back then, I didn't realize how incredibly open-minded my parents were, nor did I fully realize the depth of wisdom and grace found in Karine's straightforward answer to a child's sincere question. In my home, Keith and Howard were embraced wholeheartedly. Sadly, this was not the norm in the world at large. As many of us know, homosexuality in the sixties was left in the closet. Both Keith and Howard had served in World War II. Keith had been a Major stationed in London. Howard was one of the first amphibious soldiers to land on Omaha Beach in Normandy that historical day of June 6, 1944. He bravely led a troop of 200 men. My entire life, I have never understood the controversy around allowing homosexuals in the military. Here were two amazing gay men who had served their country in the military with honor and dignity. I saw nothing wrong with that. All I saw were two great people who loved each other.

Nor have I ever understood why skin color is used to separate people and keep communities segregated. In our home, blacks and whites lived and worked together harmoniously. Karine was my second mother, the one person I could turn to and ask absolutely anything in the world. Elsa, who was married, came by our house twice a week to iron everything from our bed sheets to Dad's starched white shirts to my white underpants. She was genuinely nice and pleasant to be around. The first time I saw AJ, he was raking leaves in our yard. Later that day he washed our windows and then picked me up from school, wearing his snazzy chauffer's cap. It always tickled me to see him in that fancy cap.

Mom, Dad, Will, Matt, Karine, AJ, Elsa, Keith, Howard, Scout, and me, the baby of the bunch—we were one big extended family. Some of us lived in our Japanese dream house in Memphis, others came by to work, but while there, our hearts were sheltered from cruelties and the irrationality of the outside world by acres of gardens and rich woods. In my child eyes, our home was not very different from the beautiful realm Karine described to me as the Heaven just inside the pearly gates.

I had amazing people in my life and an upbringing that many people envied.

But you know, things aren't always as they appear, are they?

CHAPTER TWO

THE SAD TRUTH
ABOUT FUNNY BREATH

Funny breath runs rampant on both sides of my family. I don't know where the term comes from, but "funny breath" has become my code phrase for the alcoholism that has attacked one generation after another, bringing chaos, heartbreak, and in many cases, a beautiful life cut way too short. Dad is the only man from his family, going back many generations, who made it past his fifties. His father, brothers, and sister all fell victim to liver disease. Very few of my relatives escaped the devastating spell of the demon that dominated my lineage. And then there came a time when I fell under the curse of that demon, too. But that story comes later ...

Dad's tenacity and penchant for hard work kept alcohol from ruining his achievements. Perhaps his drive to succeed came from my grandfather. In 1952, at the age of 54, Grandfather succumbed to liver disease, but before passing away, he entrusted Dad with his flourishing automobile business. By the age of 23, Dad was running the largest automobile dealership in Memphis—in fact, the largest in the Mid-South. I genuinely believe that Grandfather and Dad had a relationship defined by respect and admiration.

Discipline was a trait Dad developed early on. Grandmother and Grandfather sent him away to a college prep boarding school in Indiana with a long, rich heritage. Since Grandfather never had the chance to get a complete education, he wanted his sons and daughter to have the best possible. For four years Dad excelled at the prep school; he was a brilliant student, particularly in mathematics, a natural learner who rarely had to open a book.

Grandmother was a strong woman. I don't think she had an affectionate bone in her body. Maybe the challenges of her early life had something to do with this. Her parents were Scottish immigrants who settled in upstate New York and worked as laborers. Grandmother worked as a servant for a wealthy Scottish family. When she turned 27 in 1920, she hopped on a train and headed west for New Mexico. Without a doubt she was a woman with gumption, a woman armed with independence, energy, and a desire to explore the world.

But when Grandmother arrived in Kansas City, she met Grandfather, a handsome policeman in neighboring Independence, Missouri. She never did make it to the Land of Enchantment. Instead, she and Grandfather married and she settled into the life of a Midwesterner. Grandfather loved being a member of the police force. He patrolled the street where Harry S. Truman sold men's clothing at a haberdashery he ran with a colleague long before becoming the 33rd president of the United States. Earlier in life Grandfather had been a mule trader and had served in World War I. His parents were German immigrants who settled in Missouri and had ten children—five boys and five girls. Since they had very little money, Grandfather didn't have the chance to get an education beyond the sixth grade.

Grandfather's photos reveal a dashing man, tall and well-built with dark brown hair, a fair complexion, and piercing brown eyes. In one particular photo his 6'3" frame straddles one of his thoroughbred horses. That full-grown horse looks about the size of a dachshund beneath him!

I have been told that women adored him and men hated him. I have also been told that he was the perfect paradigm of a host, genteel and proper to his guests. And I have been told he didn't start drinking until he was around 50. Hard to believe, but that demon took him within four years. Let this serve as a warning— alcoholism can strike at any stage of life.

After Grandfather and Grandmother married, they faced an immense challenge. It was the 1930s, the era of the Great Depression when countless families struggled to stay afloat. Always one to take risks, Grandfather ended up losing a 4,000-acre farm in Tennessee in a poker game. To redeem himself, he knew he would have to look for new ways to generate income. One day, a friend told him that the automobile business could be lucrative. Grandfather borrowed a total of $3,000 from his two sisters, Ana and Eva, and set out to build his business.

Money in hand, he and Grandmother moved to Denver, Colorado where he established his first dealership. Grandmother gave birth to four children—three sons and a daughter. But the Centennial State was not to be their permanent home. Grandfather was offered a franchise in Memphis, and so the family moved in 1938 to the city on the bluff that rises from the mighty Mississippi River. Business boomed. Grandfather had struck gold.

When Dad took control of the business, he expanded it west towards the Pacific Ocean, opening a Chevrolet dealership in Beverly Hills, California. He had accomplished this ambitious expansion during his early twenties. Clearly, his business sense was impeccable. Dad had ambition, know-how, drive. Others in their youth might have mishandled the enterprise, losing everything in the process, but not Dad. Armed with discipline and confidence, he pushed forward, growing the business year after year.

And Dad had a knack for brushes with fame. In the 1950s, before entering the Army, Elvis Presley approached my father to ask if he could play his guitar in Dad's used car dealership.

Without hesitation, Dad replied, "No."

Though he didn't say this next part to Elvis' face, I later heard him say that he didn't want a "greasy-haired, tight-jeaned guitar player" on the lot. Can you believe it? Only country singers were allowed.

Despite Dad's savvy business sense, it had never been his dream to become a businessman. Dad wanted to be a math professor. He was working toward his degree when Grandfather pulled him out of college; he needed his son for the business. Perhaps he knew he wouldn't be around much longer. Though Dad never had the chance again to pursue his math professorship dream, his keen business dealings were all about numbers.

Grandmother was a prominent figure in my life. Sundays were spent at her home, a Greek Revival colonial-style house on acres of land where exotic peacocks roamed freely and streams meandered between blooming magnolia trees and azalea bushes. The rooms of her home looked like eighteenth-century French rococo salons with pale blue fabric wallpaper displaying flora and fauna designs. An ornate chandelier embellished the ceiling above the dining table, and silver candelabras adorned the buffet table. Most of her furnishings were exquisite antiques. After church, Dad would take Mom, Will, Matt, and me to spend the afternoon and evening with Grandmother. We had a midday dinner, which was formal, and an evening supper, which was more casual (though the word "casual" at Grandmother's house was an oxymoron) with T-bone steaks. When we finished eating, we'd watch some television: "The Wonderful World of Disney" at 6 p.m., "The Ed Sullivan Show" at 7 p.m., and Bonanza at 8 p.m.

It was at Grandmother's that I saw The Beatles' first appearance on "The Ed Sullivan Show." The date was February 9, 1964. I wasn't quite ten years old. I sat cross-legged on the floor in absolute awe of Paul, John, George, and Ringo as they sang "She Loves You" and "I Want to Hold Your Hand."

I have so many other memories of being at Grandmother's home. Thanksgiving and Christmas with all the cousins—all fourteen of us! The warmth of her home after coming in from the chilling cold air, garland and ornaments lining her sweeping staircase; the smell of turkey and dressing (bread dressing, of course, since Grandmother was a Yankee); and Grandmother in the kitchen giving her black servants, Robert and Beatrice, orders with politeness and authority. Under the dining table a bell hid next to Grandmother's right foot, concealed by the Oriental rug. It was her way of discreetly letting the kitchen staff know they were needed. On cue, Robert would enter the dining room, dressed in a black suit and bowtie. With utmost professionalism, he would bring us an array of delicious food served on sterling silver platters that he handled expertly.

Grandmother's home was magical during the holidays. She had the most beautiful flocked Christmas tree, decorated with blue ornaments and clear lights, mounds of perfectly-wrapped presents underneath. Outside, the snow-covered ground, icicles hanging from the rafters, the frozen lily pond, and Grandmother's flock of peacocks served as the perfect backdrop. Those peacocks would stand at the parlor door, looking in all too knowingly!

Ancient folklore has it that two peacocks sit at the Gates of Heaven. In my art history studies many years later I learned that the peacock is the Christian symbol of eternal life. In Greco-Roman myths, the circles on a peacock's plumage are the vault of Heaven, the "eyes" of the stars. If this is the case, those peacocks saw an awful lot going on at Grandmother's home! Through a large bay window that overlooked the snow and frozen pond, those beautiful birds would stare at my cousins and me as we tore into our Christmas presents. I was mesmerized by those creatures. I loved watching them strut around the acreage confidently, showing off their exquisite emerald green and deep blue plumage.

Spring is my favorite season, perhaps because my birthday is in April. Mom always had white birthday cakes made for me, either in the shape of a bunny or an Easter basket covered in pink and yellow flower blossoms made of icing. On Easter Sunday all of us cousins got together, ten boys and four girls. The girls dressed in white smocked dresses and the boys wore white shorts and shirts with bowties. Year after year we hunted for eggs, which were filled with quarters, one-dollar bills ... and even five-dollar bills! All of us clutched our baskets as we raced and pushed and shoved.

Grandmother never failed to look stately and proper. When she went out, she wore her mink stole at all times. She even attended an Elvis concert in 1974, second row center seat, wearing that mink stole of hers. Grandmother loved Elvis. She had quite an affinity for music, for travel, for culture. She was a woman who had circled the world on the most elegant of cruise ships. And yet, through it all, Grandmother was a deep mystery to me.

She was not a person one could easily get close to. I never saw her hug Dad or anyone in our family, for that matter; and I certainly never heard "I love you" come out of her mouth. With her prim and proper demeanor, she commanded respect. And that is exactly what each of us gave her.

In later years, as Memphis grew eastward, the city contacted Grandmother about purchasing her property to construct highways. They succeeded in buying most of the land around Grandmother's home. In the end, only her house and a few surrounding acres remained. Her home became an island between two highways. But she never budged. Until the very end, she had gumption.

She died in that home in 1987 at the age of 94, having outlived her husband and three of her four children. Today, no trace is left of that exquisite home that was such a major part of my young life.

How is it possible that Grandmother outlived three of her four children? Well, all of them had funny breath, which eventually ended up killing them.

I remember watching Dad and his two brothers pull out flasks from their jackets to take sips of hard liquor. As a child, I was befuddled as to what they were drinking. Dad's sister would frequently excuse herself and slip away to her upstairs bedroom. That's where she hid her bottles. Grandmother did not allow alcohol in the house, but somehow plenty of it snuck in. That demon took each one of their lives—one at the age of 44, and two in their mid-fifties—just as it had taken Grandfather's. Amazingly, Grandmother never had a drink in her entire life.

Dad was the sole survivor of that family for thirteen years, the only child who outlived his mother. But his last ten years were not quality ones. Heart failure ultimately took his life.

Mom grew up in a small country town in central Tennessee. Her dad, Harry, was a postal carrier. But he was Papa to me.

In the early days, he would deliver the mail on his mule, his mailbag always full of candy for the kids. In the 1940s, items like gas, meat, and sugar were rationed due to the ongoing war. As a mail carrier, Papa had access to more gas ration stamps. And thanks to these vital ration stamps, Mom was one of the few teenagers with a drivable car. It was a Dodge convertible, one of the very first models. With just the turn of a switch, the top lifted open and folded at the back of the car. Rumor has it Mom almost pulled out the windshield once because she forgot to unlatch the front before putting the top down!

Everyone in town loved Papa. He was good-looking, charming, and funny. He used to leave an orange and an apple inside every mailbox on his route at Christmas, and he enjoyed singing in a barber-shop quartet. There was no question as to how he managed to catch the eye of Ethel, a beautiful 17-year-old ten years his junior with striking jet-black hair and pearly white skin. They married, and my Gramma Ethel gave birth to Mom in 1926. Everyone in town loved Ethel, even though she had a bit of a stubborn streak. She had a huge heart for babies, so if a new mom couldn't nurse her newborn child, she stepped up to the task. Her breasts had enough milk to accommodate practically the entire county!

Papa, too, was an alcoholic. Gramma Ethel left him after Mom graduated from high school in 1944. Mother and daughter headed to Memphis, the big city on the mighty Mississippi, to build a new life. Though Gramma Ethel had sworn Papa off completely, for years she would not grant him a divorce. I never quite understood why that was, but I think her unwillingness to fully release him made her feel as if she had a certain level of control over him.

Mom's second cousin TJ paid for her to attend college in Memphis. He also procured a simple brown-brick, one-bedroom apartment for Gramma Ethel and Mom to live in. Gramma Ethel worked two full-time jobs. During the day she was a salesperson at Broadnax Jewelry, and at night she worked in the post office. She had no choice but to work around the clock.

Mom often took Will, Matt and me to visit with her side of the family, simple country folk who prided themselves on hard work. My great-grandparents, Ida and Elmer (he died before my brothers and I were born), owned a cotton gin and a rustic, antiquated, white-board general store. Will, Matt, and I relished going to that old store, which had everything a kid would love: a pot-bellied stove, coca-colas, and hard gumballs. It was right across the road from Great-Grandmother Ida's house, a simple A-framed wooden house painted white. She would sit on her porch rocking in her chair slowly and deliberately, waiting for us as she chewed snuff and spat into a tin can. She was a petite woman, quite hunched over in her old age, but beneath the surface was a woman of strength. You could see it in her piercing blue eyes that seemed to see right through you.

In those days Ida didn't have a bathroom in her house, so we had to go to the outhouse, which was basically an enclosed simple bench and hole. But we didn't care. This was Ida's home. This was a world where people moved slowly and worked hard.

Papa often came to visit us in Memphis. It was his nature to be cheerful and in good spirits, and I loved seeing him. He had a pet crow named Kaka who was always perched on his shoulder. He sure loved that bird. Some weekends, Will and Matt traveled to visit Papa, who lived at Miss Macy's, a guest home. Mom and Dad would put my brothers on a train at Buntyn, the station on Southern Avenue in Memphis, and send them up north. It's the same station where Mom and Dad put me on the train four consecutive summers to attend Camp Sequoia in Bristol Virginia, for six weeks at a time, where I "mastered" the art of archery, marksmanship and synchronized swimming, but dreaded the weekly Sunday weigh-ins.

Will, Matt and Papa often ate fried chicken dinners at the hotel right across from Miss Macy's. During the fifties and early sixties this hotel was run by two sisters, Flossie and Bertha. It was the prime eating spot in town known for having the best fried chicken in all of central Tennessee! The large restaurant could accommodate huge groups like the Rotary Club and the Lions Club. Then there was the bar that Papa liked to frequent. He would take Will and Matt with him, leave them in his car, and re-emerge from the bar several hours later. Will and Matt didn't think anything of it. That was Papa, and we all loved him.

A neat freak, he never left the house in anything other than a freshly pressed white shirt and slacks, along with a brown hat with black trim. Since Miss Macy's had only one bathroom, Papa would always cover the toilet seat with tissue whenever Will or Matt had to use the lavatory.

As neat as he was, Papa could not hide the beer cans underneath his bed. Will remembers seeing them. He also remembers the time Papa visited us one weekend. Papa went outside near the trash cans and started drinking until he passed out. Furious, Mom kicked him out of the house, yelling at him to sober up. Even when he tried to slow down, tried to have just one beer, it never seemed to work for him. If Papa had one beer, it would inevitably turn into a six-pack, or more. He didn't know how to stop.

Though I was never on those adventures with Will and Matt, I do remember many times when I ate fried chicken with Papa at the hotel, and I do remember Papa's room at Miss Macy's, though I never stayed there overnight. Mom always accompanied me on our visits. How I wish I had had the chance to know Papa more.

Later in life, Papa met Miss Ruth, a kind, stoic woman who took good care of him. With her help, he accomplished what he had up to that point failed to do: He sobered up and never touched alcohol again. He hired an attorney to grant him a divorce from Gramma Ethel, and he married Miss Ruth. She was sweet to my brothers and me. I especially remember the delicious strawberry cakes Miss Ruth baked us whenever we visited.

Papa died in 1975 of a heart attack while shaving. He was 79 years old. I was in college at the time. At his funeral, I remember looking down at him in his casket. He lay there, holding his hat in his hands, all the tension in his face washed away by a kind of gentle peace. He was my first loved one to pass away.

Gramma Ethel was a strong presence in my life. She was at our house most of the time, and when she wasn't at our place, I often stayed with her at her apartment.

She had strong affection for me, often endearingly calling me "Piss-Ain't" (a true Southernism!). I loved her dearly and was happy to have her as part of our household while I was growing up.

Up until I went off to college, Gramma Ethel always scratched my back. "Come here," she'd say, stretching out her fingers and motioning in front of her. My eyes always lit up when she did that. I'd eagerly position myself with my back facing her, and she'd get right to work with those long nails against my back. I'd close my eyes and get lost in the feeling of it. It was so calming. I guess it's no surprise that I always scratched the backs of my children, Savannah and Steven, as they were growing up. I wanted them to enjoy the same luxury Gramma Ethel graciously offered me.

I thoroughly enjoyed Florida vacations with my family when I was a little girl. They were bliss-filled days of sun and relaxation and light breezes. Almost every day, we'd venture into the water. Gramma Ethel would stand waist-high in the ocean as she held me in her arms. Whenever waves moved closer and closer toward us, my heart pounded in my chest with nervous anticipation. I was terrified, but excited all the same. I knew that I was safe in Gramma Ethel's arms. She'd never let anything happen to me.

"Ready? They're coming," she would tell me as she eyed the approaching waves and clutched me tightly. My breath would catch in my throat as I braced myself. The waves always came fast and hard, knocking into us with such force. Gramma Ethel and I squealed in delight!

There was something so carefree and spirited about my Gramma Ethel. Savannah and Steven loved spending time with her when they were little. She always baked the most delicious rolls and cakes. And when my children were toddlers, she let them run around naked in her apartment.

"Babies just need to have their butts aired out," she would tell me, a half-serious look on her face.

Ironically, later in life Gramma Ethel developed funny breath, too. Though alcohol had wreaked havoc upon her marriage, she nevertheless succumbed to it. It began when I was still a child, but I did not realize it then. Many evenings she would sit in our kitchen, alone on the barstool, nursing a drink. Years later I learned she was having a shot of whiskey. As I often did whenever I needed a trustworthy person to turn to with my most pressing questions, I sought Karine.

"Why does Gramma Ethel sit there every night alone?"

"Oh honey, she's just relaxing," Karine replied gently, never one to judge others. "She's been on her feet all day." My dear Karine knew how close my grandmother and I were. She would never say anything to jeopardize the special bond we shared. For a time, Karine's loving answer was sufficient.

Gramma Ethel's condition worsened as the years passed. One morning, when I was a young mother, I found her with a black eye and blood dripping down her nightgown. In a drunken stupor, she had fallen and bruised herself badly. As I stared in sadness and disbelief, my left hand clutched Savannah's little hand and in my right arm I held onto Steven. From that point on I knew I could no longer leave my children in her care. That's the thing about funny breath: it only worsens as time goes by.

"She can't stay in that apartment on her own anymore," Mom told me.

"So, what're you thinking?" I asked.

"A nursing home, maybe," came Mom's reply, her eyes distant.

"A nursing home?"

To me, that didn't seem like the right thing to do. I objected, but Mom kept quiet the rest of the conversation. She had made up her mind.

Soon after, Mom placed Gramma Ethel in a nursing home back in central Tennessee. Though I knew my grandmother had family there and would not be alone, it still upset me. We were the ones closest to her. But there was nothing I could do to change the situation.

Oddly enough, Gramma Ethel outlived Mom by four years, dying at the age of 85 in 1994. Right before she passed, I visited her. She looked so thin and pale lying in that hospital bed. Not only was she suffering from the ravages of alcohol and emphysema, she was also suffering from a broken heart. After Mom died, Gramma Ethel was never the same. A huge part of her very being had been ripped away, a part she had relied upon for years.

Matt and I made funeral arrangements for our grandmother. We had her buried in Memphis next to Papa. It was what she had wanted, that and a small, simple memorial with family and a few close friends. I will never forget the moment Steven, who was nine at the time, stood and read a letter he wrote to Gramma Ethel, telling her how much he loved her and making sure to mention her delicious homemade rolls. Few words were spoken at the ceremony. I think we all simply knew she was content to leave this earth and join her only child and the only man she had ever loved.

As with Gramma Ethel it took Mom a while to develop funny breath. It wasn't until her forties that she began to drink on a regular basis. Before then she had not been much of a drinker, having only a beer now and then. But as the years passed, the drinking increased. I don't know what led her to embrace the bottle, but I suspect it had something to do with a past marked by loss and heartbreak. Mom was a teenager during World War II. Many of her friends went off to war and never returned. The whole nation was devastated by the loss of so many of its young people, but somehow America continued to press forward, to move beyond the destruction.

After attending college for a couple of years, Mom dropped out and became a flight attendant for American

Airlines, working on a route between Memphis and New York City. This was a big deal; in the 1940s, being a flight attendant was equivalent to being a model or a beauty queen contestant. Attendants had to meet very precise height and weight requirements. Only the most beautiful, charming, and engaging women were hired. On not so rare occasions, Mom would hide Papa in the bathroom of the plane during take-off so he could travel to NYC with her! I guess family members had no flying privileges back in the 1940s.

While working as a flight attendant, she met an Air Force pilot seven years her senior. They married in 1946, soon after WWII ended. Mom was 20 and he was 27. And do you know that Will, Matt, and I never knew this until we were in our thirties? Gramma Ethel told my husband Paul. He relayed the news to me and I passed it on to my brothers. Not one of us was shocked, though. We just wondered why this "secret" was kept from us. When I told Mom I knew of her past marriage, she simply dismissed it and changed the subject—some things were simply left unsaid.

When I think back to my childhood, I recall Gramma Ethel showing me a photograph of a good-looking man and saying that he was an old boyfriend of Mom's. I never thought twice about it. Only in retrospect do I realize this man was her first husband.

The story was that after marrying this pilot, Mom moved to South Carolina to start a new life with him. Their marriage was annulled within a year. If I had to guess, I'd say the reason was Gramma Ethel. Mom had a relationship with her that no one could touch—a love/hate relationship, a relationship of control, but they couldn't live without each other. After Gramma Ethel left Papa, Mom was all she really had. When this pilot took Mom to South Carolina, Gramma Ethel probably intervened somehow.

It still amazes me that Mom kept this secret from my brothers and me for so many years. Dad always knew. After Mom died, was I surprised when this gentleman called me! Our conversation went like this:

"Hello."

"Hi, is this Bethany Ann?"

"Yes."

"Bethany Ann, my name is Henry. I was your mom's first husband."

Silence. I felt my heart pounding wildly. He knew my name. How had he gotten my number?

Finally and a bit hesitantly, I replied softy, "Oh, hi."

Then very quietly, with the nicest Southern accent, he said, "Bethany Ann, I heard your mom passed away and I wanted you to know how sorry I am."

"Thank you."

"I am calling you, not Will or Matt," he continued, and I was startled that he knew their names as well, "because I thought I would feel more comfortable speaking with Jo Ann's daughter. I don't know what you have heard about me, but I want you to know I am not a bad man. I loved your mom very much. I was crazy about her. You know, at the time we were young and it was hard for her living apart from family." I knew he meant Gramma Ethel. He continued, "She was constantly commuting between Memphis and South Carolina. That was hard on our marriage. I finally told her that she either stay with me in South Carolina or go home. She chose to move back to Memphis, and I certainly understood. I did remarry. She, too, has passed away."

My mind processed what he'd just shared, and I thought, *Bad man? Why would I think that?* I had only recently discovered that Mom had been married before. I didn't know a thing about him. I didn't know why they divorced. I really didn't know anything about the marriage!

"Oh, I am so sorry," I replied.

"Ethel and I have kept in touch. She sent me photos of you, Will, and Matt. I know how much your dad loves your mom and that he took very good care of her."

How does one respond to this? "Thank you," I replied simply. Then I told Henry how nice it was to talk with him, and we finished our conversation. I got off the phone with tears in my eyes, wondering about this gentleman, about Mom's past. In my heart I believe Mom always held a special place for him in her heart.

A few days later I told Dad that Henry had called. He looked into my eyes and said, simply and softly, "Good."

That was that.

In the world where I grew up, people hid behind walls. They insulated themselves from all that was unpleasant and painful. They insulated themselves from the truth. They thought they had to do this in order to maintain appearances. And so they kept secrets, burying the past deep inside, carving out a private place that no one else could touch. In every family there are secrets. As children, we grow up not fully realizing the extent of all those things that lie just beneath the surface.

Looking back on it, the veil of secrecy was probably intricately tied to the alcoholism that ran rampant through both sides of my family. With a few drinks, one could drown sorrows and numb feelings. One could anesthetize all the regrets, the unspoken words, the undesirable realities.

I remember going over to some of my friends' homes in the afternoon after school and seeing their moms always with cocktails in hand. I was so used to seeing this that it actually went unnoticed until I began reflecting on my past many years later. These women had a role to play, a role that adhered to society and country club standards. Perhaps they did not have much of a choice. Many stayed in marriages they just could not untangle themselves from. Alcohol numbed the pain.

Of course men bore their own challenges. They were the heads of their families. They had a certain level of responsibility, providing for their wives and children. And appearances during that era seemed to be the most important criteria. Husbands drank, wives drank, and somehow it seemed chic.

Don't get me wrong. I'm not justifying turning to alcohol to detach from problems, not at all. I am merely pointing out that this explanation sheds some light on why many people found (and continue to find) such comfort in drinking, albeit false comfort.

As for myself, there are numerous reasons why I began abusing alcohol. Certainly genetics played a large factor. But more significantly, I know it was tied up with my insecurity, my lifelong feeling of not being good enough. I guess one never really knows exactly why — what initially begins as a fun pastime becomes a hellish nightmare of spiraling down into an abyss.

CHAPTER THREE

CAN'T SEGREGATE
UNCONDITIONAL LOVE

"Miss Bethany Ann, it's seven o'clock. Time to get up."

For thirteen years, those familiar words came drifting out of the intercom. Those familiar words repeated by that comforting voice, Karine's voice. Somehow everything she said sounded like a melody, a set of sweet notes that rose and fell in perfect succession.

Each morning I would drag myself out of bed, get dressed, and begin my walk down the long hallway of travertine floor that seemed to stretch endlessly toward the kitchen. The smell of fried eggs and bacon crackling on the stove wafted through the air, beckoning me forward. The intoxicating aroma shifted me out of my sleepy state, propelling me closer and closer to the source. As I neared the kitchen, I always heard Karine humming a tune, a tune about God. Everything Karine did was to the glory of the Lord, whether cooking fried chicken and okra, cleaning the house, or taking good care of me.

Even today, when I hear any version of the gospel "Peace in the Valley," I hear only Karine's voice:

> *Oh well, I'm tired and so weary*
> *But I must go along*
> *Till the Lord comes and calls, calls me away, oh yes*
> *And the morning's so bright*
> *And the lamb is the light*
> *And the night, night is as black as the sea, oh yes*
> *There will be peace in the valley for me, some day*
> *There will be peace in the valley for me, oh Lord I pray*
> *There'll be no sadness, no sorrow*
> *No trouble, trouble I see*
> *There will be peace in the valley for me, for me*

(Adapted from original lyrics written by Thomas Dorsey)

When I hear in my mind her sweet, strong voice, I see, if only for one fleeting moment, Karine holding the hand of that uncertain little girl with the soft, strawberry-blonde curls and chubby legs. The two of us are facing the heavens, and Karine is belting out note after beautiful note. This image fills me with such peace. I am still, and will always be, eternally humbled by this vision, eternally grateful for Karine.

In the afternoons when I got home from school, Karine was usually in the kitchen making chocolate chip cookies and preparing the evening supper. As soon as I opened the sliding kitchen doors I could smell those glorious cookies. Karine looked so professional in her crisp, white uniform, pacing through the kitchen with a certain command, a sense of authority, busying herself with various tasks. When not cooking or doing her household chores, she would be in her bedroom, a small but comfortable room just off the kitchen.

When the school bell rang at three in the afternoon, I would get so excited about spending the afternoon watching TV with Karine. "The Beverly Hillbillies" was our favorite program. She and I would sit on her bed and laugh hysterically over the Clampetts' antics, their cement pond, and especially Granny stirring her infamous possum stew. I have never known anyone who laughed as genuinely as Karine did. Her entire face absolutely radiated as she released sounds of utter elation.

When we weren't watching TV, we were either playing "The Beverly Hillbillies" board game or simply reading quietly, side by side, Karine with the Holy Bible, me with a schoolbook. One of the most amazing things Karine taught me was the beauty of just being. Here was a woman who, in my mind, was untouched by the unfair treatment she often received due to others' reactions to her skin color. Now that I am years older, I am certain that the way some people treated Karine hurt her deeply. But I don't recall ever seeing a trace of anger, bitterness, or even resentment in her. This is true grace. This is how she chose to live her life. She was one of the most joyous people I have ever known.

Sometimes Karine would take me to the Memphis Zoo. That was such a treat! The zoo was located in Midtown, about thirty minutes from my home. Not far at all, but for a child, of course, a thirty-minute car ride is an eternity. At the zoo, Karine would hold my hand as we wandered from cage to cage, peering in at all the animals. Though I was fascinated to see the various creatures, I always felt a tinge of sadness. It seemed wrong to have them docile and caged up like that. I wanted them to be free.

My most prevalent memory, though, is not about the animals. It's about the drinking fountains and snack bars. Segregation was carried out in full force. We had no choice in the matter: Karine would sip water from one fountain, and I would sip from another. Karine would order a snack from one window and I from another.

"Go on, honey, you get your snow cone from the window on the other side," Karine would urge me warmly, as if it was the most natural thing in the universe.

Hesitant at first, I did just as I was told. I went on my own to stand in the line that was designated for white people. From across the way, as she stood in her line, Karine never took her eyes off me. Though this was always the routine, I never did get used to it. I felt very uncomfortable leaving Karine's side. We belonged together. This forced segregation was pointless.

But what I learned from Karine was priceless: I learned about unconditional love. Society can force conditions upon people based on skin color or other arbitrary criteria, needless conditions that stem from arrogance, ignorance, elitism, and prejudice. But an open heart will never fully accept these restrictions. That's what Karine and I had—big, open hearts. She stood in her line, I stood in mine, but we were never separate. Love bound us together.

Some Saturday mornings, Karine would put on her finest dress and hat and take me downtown with her. Though I never liked putting on my "Sunday best" I was thrilled to take these trips, excited to browse department stores with her and watch barges roll along the Mississippi.

Getting downtown meant a bus ride. Every time we hopped on, Karine asked if I wanted to sit in the front of the bus with other white people. Every time, I shook my head. I always chose to sit in the back with her and the black people in the "Colored Section." With a calm, even expression on her face, Karine would lead me all the way to the back, every pair of eyes, black and white, following us with rapt attention.

When we sat down, Karine would hold my hand and look over at me to make sure I remembered my manners. Often she would say, "Now, Miss Bethany Ann, sit nice and proper, and put your hands in your lap." All the passengers shot us funny looks and whispered amongst themselves during the entire ride. I knew they were talking about us, but I didn't care. I knew I was safe. I was with Karine.

One day, Karine and I made our way to the back of the bus, just as we had done countless times before. We passed a "proper" elderly white woman who stared at us sternly. Loud enough for me to hear, she whispered to a woman sitting next to her, "That child, I believe, is the daughter of that rich, young car dealer who lives in that mansion out east. What is she doing on the bus with her colored maid?"

Her tone was disapproving and sharp. I stared at her evenly as we walked past, wondering how a stranger could sit there and pass judgment on my family, on Karine, on me. She didn't know us. She had no clue what Karine and I had. Instead of feeling rattled, I merely felt sorry for this small-minded, bitter woman. It was not the first time I had heard a comment like that. Nor would it be the last. Each time, I simply stared back. These people did not know what they were saying. I knew I had absolutely nothing to worry about. I was under no threat of any kind. Karine's presence offered a comfort unlike anything I have ever known.

Some Sundays Karine took me to her church in Mississippi, followed by a blissful afternoon of fishing at a lake designated for black people. I loved going to her church. It was a simple wooden building in desperate need of a paint job, its defining feature an unadorned steeple. Instead of sitting on cushioned pews, parishioners sat on hard benches. But it wasn't about the furnishings; here, the church truly was about the people, and each Sunday morning the building came to life with music and vitality as voices soared and bodies swayed.

Even inside the church, the Southern humid air was so suffocating that I felt myself perspiring and searching for air. All around us, women dressed in their Sunday best fanned themselves with rapid motions, trying desperately to cool down. Beads of sweat ran down the faces of the men, who were dressed in coats and ties. Yet despite the physical discomfort of being there, nobody complained.

In all my life, I had not seen so much enthusiasm. My ears had never before heard so much singing and praising God. Bodies swayed and danced with care-free abandon, arms waved freely toward the skies, as if reaching for something bigger than words could ever express. Women exclaimed "Hallelujah" and "Amen," the words vibrating forcefully from their vocal cords. There was no doubt about it: Jesus' presence was definitely felt in that room!

One of my absolute favorite parts of the service was when the choir gave its soulful rendition of "Let Us Break Bread Together:"

Let us break bread together on our knees
Let us break bread together on our knees
When I fall on my knees
With my face to the rising sun
Oh Lord, have mercy on me

—African-American Spiritual

Every time I heard the choir sing these beautiful words, I got goose bumps. As the all-black choir praised the Lord, I wondered what they thought about a little white girl staring at them wide-eyed.

Sitting quietly next to Karine, I took in the scene around me with fascination and wonder. Many times I caught people looking curiously back at me. After a while most of the churchgoers began to realize that I was a permanent fixture on Karine's hip! For the most part, I don't think anyone minded me being there. But just like on the bus, there were some who objected to the mixing of races. I remember a particular Sunday when a woman approached Karine, her forehead scrunched up in concern and her eyes squinted to narrow slits. "Miss Karine, why do you continue to bring that white child to our church? The rest of us don't bring the children we work for."

Karine simply smiled and, without hesitation, replied, "I love this child as if she were my own. Plus, it isn't any of your business, so just run along now." I smiled up at her. After that incident, no one ever dared ask her such a question again.

When the service was over, it was time to go fishing! We changed our clothes, grabbed our fishing poles, and headed out to the muddy lake. Poles in hand, we waded through the water barefoot with our jeans rolled up to our knees, not giving much thought to the snakes that could possibly nip at our feet, although I always got a reminder.

"Honey, be careful of them snakes," Karine would tell me firmly.

"Okay, I will." And that was that.

I made sure to stay close behind Karine at all times. The black kids watched the two of us as we settled into our spot, which always was chosen depending on where Karine determined the fish were biting that day. Noticing all eyes on us, Karine and I simply looked at one another and smiled. We were used to stares. If anything, they highlighted how special our relationship was, how precious our bond.

I used to wonder what it would be like to be friends with the kids at the lake. But in that place, at that time, a white child could never be friends with a black child. It was not until I became an adult that I fully realized the significance of Karine's and my friendship. I was fortunate on many counts; Mom and Dad possessed an openness of heart and mind that allowed me to spend time with Karine in the heart of her African-American community. And Karine loved me with the tenderness and loyalty of a mother, always looking out for me first and never paying any mind to what black folk or white folk whispered to each other, or said outright to her face.

Whenever I was sick, I counted on Karine to take care of me. Sure, missing a day of school was a treat for practically any kid, but for me, having Karine home to care for me was pure heaven. I did not realize it in my childhood innocence and naïveté, but years later I figured it out—she was an angel God had sent to me!

Karine would lovingly make me chocolate milkshakes and chicken soup, food for the body and soul. Then she would sit with me in my bedroom and together we'd watch the game show "Queen for the Day," hosted by Jack Bailey and televised daily at noon. Ahead of its time, it resembled the reality shows of today with four women, each with her own sob story, vying to become Queen for the Day. The one with the saddest story won the coveted honor and was rewarded with cash, gifts, and a crown.

I had a beautiful bedroom, the kind that sparks the imagination to escape upon sweet fairy tales and happy ever-afters. Pale blue walls, drapes and bedspread embroidered with images of butterflies and flowers, a white wicker swing that hung in the corner, stuffed animals everywhere, a baby-blue parakeet that chirped from its cage, a bathtub made of hundreds of small baby-blue square tiles and large enough to spread out like angel wings, and a view of the seemingly enchanted woods where Matt and I spent so many hours of make-believe—all this created a magical world to live in. My beautiful room stirred my imagination, while Karine's maternal love warmed my heart. When she wasn't with me, she was nearby doing her household chores, and she made sure I knew she was available to me at any moment.

"Honey, if you need anything, just yell for me. I will be right with you."

Karine always treated me like a princess.

One spring afternoon, Matt had a crazy idea. He wanted to take my tiny, baby-blue parakeet out of its cage to the balcony outside my bedroom, just to see what would happen. The result transpired in about half a second. One moment the parakeet was perched in Matt's hands, and the next moment, it was gone—it just darn disappeared! Matt and I were so dumbfounded we were speechless. Neither of us expected my parakeet to go missing.

I ran to the kitchen yelling, "Karine, come look! Hurry!"

"What is it, child?" She hurried after me to my balcony where Matt was still staring into the sky. Through tears I explained what happened. With hands on her hips and eyes wide open in disbelief, she exclaimed, "Lord Jesus!"

The three of us tilted our heads to the sky, straining to hear the slightest flutter of wings. We saw nothing. My parakeet was gone for good.

I will always remember the priceless expression on Karine's face when I told her of my bird's sudden departure. Though she never said it, I could just hear the words going through her mind, "Child, what were you thinking?"

In 1956 the Supreme Court made segregation on any means of transportation unconstitutional, and in 1964 President Johnson approved the Civil Rights Act. However, discrimination still pervaded as buses remained segregated in many parts of the United States. In most cases, black people continued to have little or no opportunity to advance.

As for Karine, one of the few jobs she could get was that of a maid, despite the fact that she was educated. She took pride in her work, consistently putting in 110% effort in all she did, whether it was taking good care of me, cleaning our large house, or preparing delicious fare in our kitchen. Had the times been different, she could have been anything she wanted to be. But circumstances would not allow this, and Karine made the most of what life offered her.

I remember that tragic day when Martin Luther King, Jr. was assassinated in Memphis in 1968. All across the country a buzz of anger vibrated among African Americans who felt that their hopes and dreams had been brutally dashed before their very eyes. I saw a different reaction in Karine, though. She showed no emotion, no sign of anger, bitterness, or despair. She was part of an older generation, and like many of her white and black counterparts, she did not want to see the status quo challenged. Yes, she had tremendous respect and admiration for Mr. King, but she did not readily seek out the change that he sought to bring to the country. That was a job left for the next generation.

Karine was a strong woman. There was a deep foundation inside her, one that was tightly rooted into place with the toughest of steel. She had seen a lot in her many years on earth. Despite her hardships and pain, she had quietly persevered. She had carved out a good place for herself in the world, and she had done so with quiet dignity, always treating others the way she would have liked to be treated.

After Dr. King was shot and killed, a thick silence filled Memphis. A curfew was set for everyone. As a 14-year-old living in wealth in the white part of town, I was not thinking about civil rights. I was unaware of its significance. It was not spoken of around the dinner table, nor was it a topic of discussion in any capacity at my school. But I do vividly remember Dad taking Karine and AJ aside and telling them how sorry he was about Dr. King's passing.

The moral fiber in Dad has always struck me. One night when our family was dining at a popular restaurant we enjoyed frequenting, a black businessman walked in. All eyes turned cold as they focused upon him. The entire restaurant became so silent you could hear a pin drop.

Without hesitation, Dad stood up, walked over to the gentleman, shook his hand, and introduced himself. The businessman smiled at Dad, relieved to be received so warmly in front of disapproving patrons. Time and again, Dad taught me by example to do the right thing.

Having grown up around Karine and AJ, as well as Keith and Howard, I have never understood racial or social injustice. Why do so many people have a sense of entitlement? Why should I, a white heterosexual woman of means, think I am entitled to a freedom and an acceptance by society over these persons who, simply by their color or sexuality, are scrutinized?

Karine and AJ were such a part of my life that I could not fathom discrimination, segregation, or feeling superior to another person, even though these concepts were lived out regularly all around me. I have often wondered through the years what Karine would have done if things had been different. I never asked her about herself—where she was from, if she was ever married, if she had children, what else she might do if she wasn't working for my family. Looking back now, I wish I had asked about these and many other aspects of her life. But I was a child, and what a child sees, a child accepts. Personal questions are unnecessary.

Today I find myself wondering: What did she study in school? What were her interests? Was she ever in love? What were her passions, hopes, dreams? How selfish of me not to ask. Why didn't I ever step into her skin? Was I too young? Too comfortable? All I know is this: I can't imagine how *my* life would have been had Karine not been a part of it.

In our house, AJ had a bedroom next to Karine's. It was small and simply furnished, containing the bare essentials: a bed, chair, and closet. AJ was not a big man, but he had strong arms. He could chop off the head of a snake without hesitation. I know, because I saw him do it with my own eyes. It had happened while I was helping AJ pull weeds from the vegetable garden. He discovered a snake slithering around and chopped its head right off as if he were slicing a piece of cake! In my child eyes, he was a hero.

Just as Karine looked out for me, so did AJ. He protected me, but he also knew how to have a good time. Together we would spend many Saturday mornings watching Yogi Bear, Boo Boo, and Huckleberry Hound. AJ had a way of carving out a vivid world of make-believe. As we watched television we acted out a series of crazy antics along with the cartoon characters on the screen. AJ and I would sit on his bed for hours watching those timeless cartoons—me in my pajamas, holding onto my favorite stuffed animal of the moment, and AJ wolfing down his grits, fried ham, biscuits, and syrup, shining Dad's shoes and imitating those characters with such glee. He was especially good at Yogi Bear: "Hello Boo-Boo!"

On some Saturday afternoons during the autumn months, I would rake leaves with AJ. I can still smell the crisp, cool air of fall and feel the crackling leaves beneath my feet. I didn't mind spending hours with AJ, working in the yard. Well, he worked, while Scout and I mostly played. I would build a mound of leaves for Scout and me to run and jump into.

AJ and Scout loved one another—they were buddies. Whenever AJ was around, Scout clung to him, never leaving his side. A true protector, Scout never let anyone or anything harm AJ or me. He was constantly looking out for us both. One of the saddest days of my life came when I returned home from six weeks at summer camp and AJ told me that Mom and Dad had put Scout on a farm.

A part of me died that day. It was a decision my parents had made, and that was that. It was not until I was an adult that I learned that putting one's pet on a farm meant putting him to sleep. Scout had jumped up on one of Matt's friends, intending to play, but his claws accidentally cut deeply into him. Matt and his friend came running into the house. Mom and I were in her dressing room, where she was putting on make-up. We knew something was wrong and jumped up as soon as they entered. Blood was running down the boy's face. Horrified, Mom rushed him to the doctor.

He required about thirty stitches around his eyes. Thank goodness he healed fine with virtually no trace of the injury left. I don't know what transpired between Mom and Dad and his parents. The boy and Matt remained friends, but the decision was made to put Scout to sleep. Now old and unpredictable, he could no longer be trusted around people outside of our family. I lost a very dear friend when he left this world. No matter what, Scout will forever be my buddy.

In the afternoons AJ would pick me up from school, all decked out in his chauffeur's cap and black uniform. He looked mighty dapper! By the expression on his face I could tell he felt so proud of himself. He always waited for me in the parking lot. When the school bell rang, I'd walk over to the car and often find him taking a catnap, snoring away.

On these occasions a big mischievous smile would spread across my face. I would creep silently over to

him and yell, "AJ!" Lucky for me, he took my child-
ish prank good-naturedly. After jumping in his seat,
his eyes flying open in surprise, he'd see me standing
there and his face would break out into a smile. The
two of us would then start to laugh uncontrollably
until tears started to form.

One summer day a huge bullfrog got caught in the
drain of our swimming pool. I dove into the deep end
and saw those bulging eyes staring back at me. Did that
give me a fright! Intent upon resolving the issue, AJ, who
didn't know how to swim, put on Matt's junior-size div-
ing equipment and disappeared into the pool. After a few
moments he popped back up to the surface. His breathing was labored and his body was shaking, but in his
hands he held the remains of the bullfrog. He had to tear
that poor creature in half just to get it out, but he did it!

Simply put, AJ was nothing short of dedicated.
Instead of shying away from a challenge, AJ embraced
it, pushing aside any obstacles—as in this case, the fact
that he couldn't swim. It was in his nature to put the
rest of us first.

Sadly, AJ also had funny breath. I remember Mom
and Dad hiring and firing him five or six times because
of his drinking problem. I didn't know what his funny
breath was until much later. Mom and Dad knew, of
course, but they loved him so much they kept hiring
him back. Years later, I heard AJ was found dead alongside a street gutter. Alcoholism had killed him, too, just
as it had snuffed out the lives of so many of my relatives.

It broke my heart to learn that my dear friend had died in this manner.

It was 1985. My husband, Paul, and I had taken our young children to Memphis to visit Grandmother. Steven was a baby and Savannah was three. I decided it was time for my sweet children to meet Karine. Even though Savannah was still very young and Steven would surely not remember this encounter, I was eager for them to know the amazing woman who had touched my life so deeply.

As I drove around my childhood city, I could see clearly that change doesn't happen overnight. Decades of segregation, poverty, and oppression still had a hold on the poorest parts of Memphis, even though segregation had been outlawed long ago. As I got closer and closer to Karine's home, I noticed conditions in the streets around us deteriorate. Broken signs hung from the entrances of abandoned buildings. Trash filled the streets, with bits of paper, shattered bottles, and plastic containers strewn about in every direction. The only white people in the black section of town, Savannah, Steven and I stood out like a sore thumb. All eyes were on us as we continued to our destination.

We reached Karine's small, run-down apartment building. When my children and I got out of the car, the entire street went silent. I looked around and noticed that the children who had been playing nearby stopped what they were doing. They stared at us, their eyes full of curiosity and distrust.

I smiled at them and carried Savannah and Steven toward the front steps of Karine's unit. I knocked on the door. We waited. I could feel excitement well up in me. Then I heard the soothing sound I hadn't heard in years. That familiar soft, angelic voice answered.

"Be right there, honey."

I heard shuffling behind the door. I tightened my grip around my children in anticipation. Within moments, we heard a clicking sound. Then the door opened and Karine stood before us, as beautiful as always. Her warm eyes stared back at me; that beaming smile spread wide across her face. I was home.

I had no words. My breath caught in my throat, and tears started rolling down my face. With my children in my arms, I fell into Karine's arms.

"Oh honey child, it has been so long ..." Karine whispered as she took Steven into her arms and held Savannah and me so close, so lovingly. My little girl gave Karine the sweetest grin and threw her arms around her—it was as if she already knew her.

When we pulled out of the hug, I took a step back and studied Karine's face. She was in her late eighties now, and the creases across her forehead reflected the passage of time. Her thick, silver hair was pulled back neatly. Yet despite all the years that had gone by, she still had that glow about her, that remarkable radiance.

Karine tucked Savannah into bed for a little nap. With Steven in her arms, we headed to the kitchen where we chatted about everything under the sun.

She asked me about Mom, Dad, Will, and Matt. And for a few moments, I was that little girl with strawberry blonde curls again ...

As I looked at Karine, I remembered how she used to talk about the pearly gates of Heaven. I could still feel her strong hands lifting me up onto the kitchen counter. Could still hear the words she spoke with such assurance. Could still feel the passion beaming from her as she spoke avidly about the Lord.

Without a doubt, my connection to the Christian faith came about thanks to Karine. Though I devoted a great deal of time to the mandatory Sunday school at the church my family and I attended, it simply did not have as much impact on me as Karine and her church did. At my family's church, I read scripture, memorized the Lord's Prayer and the 23rd Psalm, and learned the words to "Jesus Loves Me" and "Onward Christian Soldiers." And though I felt highly informed in the ways of Christianity, these teachings did little to move me or touch my heart and make God and Christ come alive.

Though I do remember, with a chuckle, my family's Sunday morning routine. After Sunday school, the five of us sat in the pew for church service in the following order: Ted, Jo Ann, Will, Matt, and me, Bethany Ann. One of the pastors was never short of words in his prayers. He always began, "Let us pray."

Matt and I would bow our heads. He would pull up his blazer sleeve, and he and I would stare at his watch ...

One minute ... two minutes ... three minutes ... four minutes ... five minutes ...

Will this prayer ever end?

I am grateful that Mom and Dad made a commitment to raise Will, Matt and me in the Christian faith, but it was Karine who gave me a deep love for the Lord. The gospel out of Karine's mouth had always been gold to me. As a child, my ears eagerly drank it up, especially when she spoke of how nice Heaven will be.

"Honey, everyone waves and says 'hi' to each other, and I will have no more back aches or tired feet when I get there," she often told me.

Karine is saying 'hi' to everyone in Heaven now. Her feet and back are free of pain, and her radiance shines even brighter now that she is with the Lord. Of this I am certain. I figured out that she had left this world when her Christmas cards stopped coming. The last Christmas card I sent her came back to me with the words "No Recipient" stamped across the envelope.

The day I took Savannah and Steven to meet Karine was one of the most precious of my life. When Karine and I said goodbye after our long-desired reunion, I somehow knew it would be the last time I would ever see her again in this world.

I have no doubt AJ is with Karine in Heaven, and they're both saying "hi" to everyone. Well, maybe to everyone but each other—those two never seemed to get along. Can't say I knew why they clashed, but the memory of them bickering with each other still tickles me to this day. Maybe, as Karine always taught me, there are many rooms in Heaven. This way, they won't have to run into each other too much.

CHAPTER FOUR

GOODBYE, MEMPHIS

Segregation in the South existed well beyond racial lines. Religions were segregated as well. Growing up, I never came in contact with people of other faiths. Jews and Catholics were unknown to me; Protestants were all I knew. The world around me was filled with boundaries, barriers, seemingly immovable walls, and lines nobody dared walk across. If it hadn't been for Karine, Elsa, and AJ, I certainly wouldn't have known any black people.

Private schools in my community were no strangers to dividing people into homogeneous groups. Protestant girls studied at one school, Protestant boys at another. Catholic girls attended an all-girl parochial school; Catholic boys went to an all-male parochial school. Jewish kids went to their academy. "Interfaith" was a foreign concept.

Very specific social standards were in place in the South I knew. Everybody was expected to conform to a particular mold. If you didn't fit that mold, you were seen as somebody on the outside, someone who did not belong. And nobody wanted to "not belong." Everyone wanted to be a part of their particular group, and they did whatever it took to fit in. All things unique and different were cast off. Only conformity was embraced.

Southern girls were brought up to be proper and well mannered. I am grateful for this upbringing, but it definitely came with a downside. There were strict expectations of us: we were to graduate from high school as genteel young ladies, go to college, get married, and continue the life our parents led. It was all about being paradigm Southern belles. As sure as the Mississippi continued to flow, we were to continue propagating the rituals of Southern society. Deep inside, I knew I could not do this. Though I couldn't exactly express what it was I wanted, I knew that it was more than what I had been accustomed to. Come graduation, I knew I'd be leaving Memphis to experience a different world—at least for a few years.

At times I felt a deep emptiness that I couldn't seem to talk about, except with my dearest friend, Jane. When we were together, if only for a moment, our trepidation and fear of life beyond our insulated cocoon disappeared. She and I were inseparable from our freshman through our senior year. She was so beautiful with her long brunette hair, olive skin, and round, soulful brown eyes. Jane had a quick wit, a plethora of unending puns that rendered all of us speechless. But behind that quick wit was a quiet reserve. She was a prolific reader, gifted painter, and thoughtful poet.

Jane lived in a lovely area in Memphis complete with a pond and swans that floated languidly along. It was by this pond that she and I would sit and "solve" the problems of the world...we knew each other's thoughts so well that words were rarely needed. In 1969 Jane painted a beautiful watercolor for me. It's a painting of two little girls, their backs toward the viewer. One is brunette, the other blonde. They are walking hand in hand toward the sunset. I was so touched when Jane gave me this priceless gift. Her painting has gone with me everywhere I have lived. Today it continues to symbolize our special, everlasting friendship.

I spent twelve years at my prep school for young ladies, which was founded in 1902 by an incredible visionary who was ahead of her time. Quite the independent individual, she firmly believed that a woman should be taught to be self-reliant, to think for herself. Her whole life she remained single and devoted to her school. When she passed away in 1962, the Commercial Appeal *newspaper wrote the following about my school's founder:*

"Her interests were as wide as the world, but the focal point of her love and concern was the education of her girls ... Life glowed within her and radiated unto every life she touched."

I never knew this remarkable person, but her presence certainly permeated our daily lives.

Back in 1925, the school had opened a new site downtown. The school's new home was a Tudor cottage-style structure with window-covered walls. That's where I began my school years, entering kindergarten in September of 1959. Right from the start I began training to become a lady. Here my fingers touched the piano for the first time as my legs dangled from the piano bench, while Miss Maude stood by directing me with her stick through simple notes and scales.

Dad drove me to school each morning since his dealership was only a few blocks away. Every day he dressed in a black suit, white shirt, and black tie, a dash of Royall Lyme on his face and neck. How I love the scent of cologne. I don't understand why so few men wear it today; for me, it helped define my father. Even now the scent brings him right back.

I was always one of the first students to arrive, greeting the teacher at the front door with a curtsy and a proper, "Yes, Miss Helen." I will never forget her—the propriety, the manners she instilled in all of us. Regardless of what class we were in, we never failed to acknowledge an incoming teacher. Invariably, we would stand in unison and say, "Good Morning, Miss (teacher's name)."

On field trips to the symphony we walked single file or two by two, each girl wearing a nice dress, short white gloves, bobby socks, and black patent-leather shoes. What a sight we were! At the end of each school day, up until I was ten, Gramma Ethel picked me up. Forever etched in my mind is the image of my smiling grandmother sitting in her car, waiting with Twinkies—my favorite treat—ready for me.

It is ironic, perhaps, that incredible women like the founder of my school as well as my teachers Miss Helen and Miss Maude did not personally achieve what Southern society expected of them, and yet they were pillars of the community. How many had laughed at them or written them off because they never married? How many frowned upon their single status? And yet, these strong, independent women achieved great things in their lives. They were phenomenal educators, leaving their mark on every girl at my school. They created opportunities for us, taught us, inspired us. These talented, hardworking women showed Southern society that one doesn't have to fit the mold to do good things in this world.

In 1964, when my school moved east to a lovely place in the country, I was in the fifth grade. What a change it was. Suddenly we had access to acres and acres of grounds surrounded by trees, complete with a lake and swans, and modern brick buildings with large windows that boasted panoramic views. It was at this location that AJ would pick me up each afternoon since Gramma Ethel lived in Midtown.

My brother Matt likes to joke that he's the reason for all the good things that have happened to me! There is some truth to this, especially in the social arena. Matt was captain of his tennis team, and thanks to him I knew every team member. I even dated his biggest competitor. And I'm pretty sure he nabbed me a spot on the cheerleading squad for his all-male school, which was just down the road from my school.

I had a certain level of visibility there thanks to Matt. I was not part of the "in crowd," though. I had no interest in football or basketball, or any social events, for that matter. The idea of being a cheerleader had never even occurred to me, especially since I had my hands full working on the yearbook and taking classical piano lessons. But it was tradition for the guys at the boys' school to pick their cheerleaders, and it was a huge honor to be asked. Many girls in my class dreamed of such an honor, since it afforded a high level of status and popularity.

Here's how I found out I'd been picked: It was my sophomore year when I encountered a group of guys waiting for me outside after school. They explained that I had been chosen to be a cheerleader for next fall. Confusion stretched across my face. I narrowed my eyes and scrunched my forehead, trying hard to make sense of their message. I asked them to repeat what they had just said. They did, and I still couldn't believe it.

Soon I discovered that I was the only one in my class who had been selected. By all accounts, I was an unlikely candidate, lacking the profile, the will, and the peppy attitude for the job. I figured it must've had something to do with Matt.

Although it had never been my aspiration, cheerleading became a big part of my life for two years through football season and basketball season. To my surprise, I discovered that I enjoyed going to the games. There was an unmistakable thrill associated with being around the crowd, feeling the electricity in the air, and cheering and jumping with gusto as points were racked up and major plays were made. After a while, I didn't even care anymore that I was horrible at jumping!

The only part that wasn't so fun was when I noticed some of the girls turning against me. I felt their eyes burning holes into me as I walked in late to school every Friday morning. I was dressed in full uniform, having just come from a pep rally. I felt badly, thinking the honor should have been given to one of them instead. Nevertheless, cheerleading gave me a level of confidence I didn't even know I had.

Just as it had been during elementary school, coming home was my favorite part of the day. As soon as I'd open the door to the kitchen and see Karine's gentle face, all my cares would vanish. Many of my high school afternoons were spent sitting on Karine's bed watching television with her. These were my moments of refuge, of peace and quiet, of just being me without pretense.

I didn't spend nearly the time I would have liked with Karine. Between weekly piano lessons, cheerleading practices, working on the yearbook, and homework, the time was not there. But when I did get to be with Karine, I knew I was "home." We laughed together and enjoyed each other's company as though nothing had changed. Indeed, other than both of us growing older, nothing had changed between us. We still had that unbreakable bond, a genuine connection of the heart. We didn't even need to talk. I rarely shared details about my day or the mini dramas that took place within my school's walls. I regularly left all of this behind once I stepped foot in the house. During my afternoons with Karine, the rest of the world simply melted away.

Annual piano recitals never failed to make me both nervous and excited. Before each performance in front of an audience, I stood by waiting in my mandatory attire—as a little girl it was a white dress, white bobby socks, and black patent leather shoes. As I grew, my outfits grew in sophistication.

My final recital took place in 1972 after I graduated from high school. I had spent countless hours practicing for it as this particular recital was especially significant, not only because it was the culmination of years of patience, time, and discipline, but also because it was held on Dad's birthday. When I announced that I was dedicating this recital to him, I saw him blush. He may have been a bit embarrassed, but he did give me a big smile, which was all I needed.

This performance differed from my previous ones in that it was a solo recital. About fifty people came to hear me play the works of Beethoven, Debussy, and Rachmaninoff. One of those in attendance was Karine. I vividly remember seeing her walk in and take a seat before I began to play. Poised and confident, she sat alone, apart from everyone else. She paid no mind to those around her. Karine's focus was solely on me. She radiated a gentle calm that soothed my pre-performance nerves. I was ready to give the performance of a lifetime.

In the middle of the first movement of Beethoven's "Pathetique" sonata, my mind went completely blank. My hands hovered over those keys for what seemed like an eternity! From the corner of my eye I saw Matt in the first row, holding his hand up to his ear, waiting and wondering if he had gone deaf. The room was so silent you could hear a pin drop. Thankfully, the notes came back to me and I continued on. Matt looked on with relief.

Despite this brief lapse, I believe Miss Maude was pleased with my performance that day. She was quite a presence in my life. Even though she was small in stature—she barely reached my shoulders, and I'm 5'4"—I knew never to cross her. Strict and proper, she always wore her hair in a net and donned black granny shoes. She had a stick in her hand, ready to whack my knuckles when I messed up. But beneath her stern façade was a tender woman. I'd see it on occasion. A twinkle in her eye and kind smile emerged many times throughout my years under her tutelage. Miss Maude is the reason I developed a passion for piano. I spent an hour with her every week for twelve years! Without a doubt, she was a powerful influence in my life. She obviously kept my attention and gave me the desire to continue.

Once I left for college, I never saw Miss Maude again. And I realized, far too late, how nice it would have been to thank her for the years she dedicated to teaching me, to lighting the flame of my love and passion for classical music. Many years later, I heard she had died in her sleep, at home in bed. How I wish I could turn back the hands of time and thank her for all she'd done for me! And when I think about Miss Helen and the years she gave to my school, the years she taught me how to be a proper young lady, I regret that I never thanked her, either. Perhaps that's how it is too often in life. We are so busy living that we take people for granted until it's too late to stop and express our gratitude.

Mrs. Carney was the school librarian. She opened my eyes to the great big world out there. In the summer of 1970, when I was 16, Mrs. Carney chaperoned a handful of students on a six-week tour of eight countries in Europe, complete with a cruise on the *SS France* from New York to Le Havre. My friend Susie and I took that trip. We always did things together, from playing piano sonatas for four hands to competing in spelling bees. We spent four summers at Camp Sequoia, one summer at Chase Tennis Academy in Pennsylvania, and now we were discovering Europe.

Mrs. Carney made sure to protect us young girls. One afternoon on a sidewalk in Rome, a young Italian man started flirting with Susie and me. Mrs. Carney wasted no time. She rolled up a newspaper and chased him away. As she ran after our suitor, threatening to bop him on the head with the paper, she kept yelling, "Shoo, shoo!" Susie and I just watched in amazement and utter disbelief.

On that trip I laid eyes on Michelangelo's well-renown sculpture, "Pieta," in St. Peter's Basilica for the first time ever. Have you ever had the experience of stopping dead in your tracks in front of a work of art with such an immediacy that words can't express, a split moment when you experience God's presence so strongly you know He has spoken to you? That's the experience I had the instant I first saw the Pieta. As I gazed on this most divine, exquisite piece my knees buckled and tears welled up in my eyes. Christ, full-grown, cradled in the lap of His pure, young mother's lap, His limp body so lifeless, so at peace. It was gripping.

Michelangelo's "Pieta" was attacked with a hammer by a mentally disturbed geologist in 1972. Though this eternal masterpiece was restored, it forever will be "hidden" by a bulletproof acrylic glass. How blessed I was to have such a personal, profound experience face to face with this work of genius.

That trip opened my eyes to travel and art, passions that have lasted a lifetime. But I never did thank Mrs. Carney for taking the time to chaperone us girls and giving us the chance to see the world.

When I was a senior, my work as yearbook editor-in-chief filled many hours of my time. Each year, the book was dedicated to somebody who had served and taught at the school. Finally it was my class' turn to publicly thank someone. My co-editor and good friend, Megan, and I—we worked together so well because we practically read each other's minds—agreed to dedicate the 1972 yearbook to two individuals, Alex and Clara. Alex was the school custodian and Clara served in the cafeteria making our lunches. Both of them had worked at our school many years.

Our dedication read:

"Let your light so shine before men, that they may see your good works...These words best reflect the light shining from your eyes, the light never dimming, the light radiating from your smiles, the light falling from your helping hands, the light perhaps overlooked, but always present, the light that we could never live without...that is why we dedicate the 1972 yearbook to you, Alex and Clara."

Our dedication was revolutionary for one significant reason: Alex and Clara were black. Nobody at our white school had ever before made a yearbook dedication to black individuals. On Awards Day, Megan and I stood in the gymnasium before the student body, teachers, administrators, and family members. As I scanned the audience, I caught sight of Mom and Karine. Each of us taking a deep breath, Megan and I announced that we had dedicated the yearbook "to those who are here every day ... and have gone too long without being recognized."

We had no idea how everyone would react. But I am delighted to say that Alex and Clara were given a standing ovation after we read their dedication. In fact, Mom and Karine were the first to stand and applaud. I will never forget the looks on Clara's and Alex's faces— their smiles and their tears touched my heart. I turned to catch another glimpse of Mom and Karine in the bleachers. They were clapping enthusiastically and crying. Dressed in her crisp, white uniform, Karine stood tall and confident. Overcome with emotion, it wasn't long before I was shedding tears, too. Times were definitely changing, thank goodness.

Megan and I didn't realize it then, but we had made school history. In 2003 a book was published to commemorate our prep school's centennial. The book summarizes a hundred years in the life of my alma mater, recording notable achievements by decades. Mentioned in 1972 was the fact that at Awards Day ceremony, Megan and I dedicated the yearbook to Clara and Alex. Reading this today brings back a vivid memory that is truly humbling.

After the ceremony, Karine rushed over to me in front of everyone. With tears of joy in her eyes, she embraced me warmly. "Honey child," she said, "I am so proud of you!"

I grew up during a time of transition when both the Civil Rights and Feminist movements were heavily underway. Between 1962 and 1972, our country witnessed the assassination of President Kennedy, the rise of the Beatles, and the fashion upheaval caused by the miniskirt. There was the assassination of Martin Luther

King Jr., and in the same year in California, Democratic presidential candidate Senator Robert F. Kennedy was killed. Neil Armstrong became the first man to set foot on the moon on July 20, 1969. Vietnam War protests raged in every direction. In 1971, the 26th Amendment to the Constitution lowered the voting age to 18. Women began to enter traditional all-male colleges. In 1972, five burglars were arrested for breaking into the Democratic Headquarters in the Watergate Hotel in Washington D.C. Construction of the World Trade Center was completed.

Yes, people were yearning for more—respect, equality, freedom. Clamor and unrest bubbled in every arena. The status quo was being challenged in a major way, but still, many people resisted change. I watched events unfold around me. Though I was not old enough to fully understand everything that was happening, I could feel the change brewing. I could feel that the world was inching steadily toward a new course.

When the time came to decide which college to attend, I set my sights on a small, distinguished liberal arts college in Maine. Matt was already studying there. Just as I had followed him throughout childhood, I decided to follow him to college. There was one slight problem, though: I wasn't entirely sure I had the grades to get in. There was May Hill, a girl in my class who had applied and got accepted during the early decision period. She was a brilliant, straight-A student, but I was not. I assumed there was no way I would ever get in.

Sure, I was a cheerleader, a classical pianist, editor-in-chief of the yearbook, and a solid student, but without straight A's, would they accept me?

I applied nonetheless and come spring, I received a letter. Yes, my college of choice had accepted me! Heart pounding, I excitedly clasped the letter in my hands and re-read those beautiful words. My first thought was that my playing classical piano helped to seal the deal. Or perhaps it had something to do with Matt? I suppose I'll never know.

When I arrived on campus I experienced culture shock in a major way. For the first time in my life, I was in school with Catholics, Jews, atheists, Blacks, and Asians. There was such a rich diversity pool brimming in the hallways and classrooms. It was unlike anything I had known in the South. Here, young people from different faiths and cultures came together in an effort to learn, achieve, and grow. Even here, though, a level of segregation existed just beneath the surface.

Guys could join fraternities, but there was no equivalent group for female students. Girls could only become social members of fraternities. The black students had their own African-American house that they retreated to. And then there were the independents, students who wanted nothing to do with any organized social group.

Issues persisted between males and females. My college had been established in 1794, but it wasn't until 1971 that female students were finally admitted, ending

177 years of the school's all-male status. I was part of the second class to accept women, and the ratio was eight men to each woman. My friends back home assumed I was extremely fortunate; there would be no shortage of men, and I would surely have many candidates to choose from.

But things didn't exactly go well in the beginning. When I first arrived, I sensed a great deal of coldness, of aloofness, from many of the men whose paths I crossed. They were not interested in making eye contact. When they spoke to me, they seemed detached. After a while, I noticed that they treated other females this way, too. Our inclusion in what was once "their" school had cut deeply into their egos, altering their view of themselves. Sharing a campus with us meant acknowledging the fact that we were equal to them, and this was not something they were ready to fully accept. I noticed that professors also had a difficult time with women being on campus.

It wasn't just many of the males who made my college life challenging. I had a difficult time with a few of the females, too. Upon entering college, I decided to venture into music studies to develop my classical piano skills. Thus, I was placed in a dorm room with two other music majors. With our shared interest in music, I assumed we would all get along just fine.

But that wasn't the case.

The three of us shared a tiny room, with all of our clothing and items competing for space across every square inch. It would've been slightly bearable had I gotten along with either of them, but we clashed terribly. Both girls were similar to each other. They wore hippie-style clothes and listened to Top 40 hits while I was still listening to Dionne Warwick, Burt Bacharach, and my favorite classical composers, Debussy and Rachmaninoff, though I did fall in love with the band *America* my freshman year. To this day their song with the haunting lyrics, "I've been through the desert on a horse with no name," takes me right back to my first year in college.

There was no common ground for me to strike up a friendship with either of my roommates. In their eyes, I was a spoiled, elitist Southern belle, someone whom they had no intention of befriending. The excitement that I'd felt leaving Memphis quickly dissipated. Though I had managed to get away from the rigid ways of the South, I was miserable. I began to seriously regret my decision. Why did I leave home? Why had I chosen a college so far away?

I tried to get acclimated to my new surroundings. Maine is captivating, mesmerizing. There is something about its coast—the scents, the sand dunes, the solitude, the way that autumn lingers in the air, the way the Atlantic Ocean sets the tone. These soothed my senses, but they could not ease the loneliness inside me.

For days, my head throbbed with wistful thoughts of Memphis, my old friends, Mom and Dad, and particularly Karine's loving arms and nonjudgmental, giving

heart. Though the campus was a beautiful place, complete with pine trees and vine-covered brick buildings,
I was homesick. I didn't know what to do. I would have
traded the Atlantic for the meandering Mississippi in
a heartbeat. My stomach turned and turned as nausea
swept through my body. I wanted out. I started to wonder if maybe I wasn't as independent as I thought I was.
Perhaps my bold move was just an exercise in cockiness,
in blind arrogance. For years, I had felt diminished by
all that had been expected of me in my hometown, and
I was way too eager to break away to something new.
Well, now it seemed I was paying the price for longing
for more.

By the end of my first week, I was drowning in
homesickness. Sitting alone on a bench outside my
dorm, I looked at a blurry world through tear-filled eyes.
My mind could not take in the beauty of the campus—I
was too busy contemplating my situation, figuring out
my next move.

A petite girl with long brown hair approached cau-
tiously. She sat next to me. Her concern was almost tangible. "Are you all right?"

I looked into the biggest blue eyes I'd ever seen.
Immediately, I felt myself relax. The girl introduced
herself as Patti. She was from a small town in northern
Maine, close to the border of Canada. As I stared into
those kind eyes, words started tumbling out.

To my surprise, when I finished talking she told
me that she was in the same boat with her roommates.

Before I could respond she asked if I wanted to be her roommate. Her idea was to go to Room Services and ask if there was an empty room we could occupy.

Without hesitation, I responded, "Yes!"

We marched over to Room Services and discovered that there was one empty room available on the fourth floor. The very next day we moved into our new dorm room, and all the homesickness I'd been feeling went away for good.

Patti and I formed a friendship that has lasted a lifetime. Without her, my college experience would have been incomplete. Patti was a biology major on her way to becoming a veterinarian. She was incredibly bright and unbelievably down-to-earth, a great combination. With her help, I learned how teenagers dressed in Maine. She took me shopping at L.L. Bean where, for the first time in my life, I purchased and wore a pair of jeans.

In addition to alerting me to the ways of style, Patti served as my interpreter. Maine's Down Easterners had a tough time understanding my thick Southern accent. On one occasion, we went shopping for a record player to put in our dorm room, but the salesperson could not understand a single word out of my mouth. Patient as always, Patti stood by my side and translated for the salesperson.

During our freshman year, Patti and I were inseparable despite our different majors. On Friday nights, we would head across the campus quad, traipsing through knee-deep snow, carrying our jug of Cold Duck, to an assortment of fraternity parties. We would end each week dancing to what Patti liked to call "foot-stomping" music.

Patti and I took many road trips to her hometown, a full day's drive away. The first time we drove to her home I was in awe of everything around me; the rugged beauty of the land by the North Atlantic captivated me. It was a brand new world, complete with miles and miles of eight-foot snowdrifts along the highway. There were no other cars or buildings in sight. It was so quiet, so still. Flurries of snow cut through the wintry grey sky. After we spent hours driving from southern to northern Maine, I finally saw a speck in the distance. It was Patti's home, a simple dwelling amid acres and acres of snow-covered potato fields.

I met her parents and liked them instantly. These kind potato farmers treated me with such generosity, making sure I had a pleasant stay and ate plenty of their delicious home cooking. With Patti's family I even tried rhubarb pie for the first time, something I'd never heard of before. Though they came from an entirely different world, I felt a familiarity with them. They were good, kind, hard-working folks, not really any different from my roots on Mom's side of the family.

In the summer of 1998, Patti and I—still close after all those years—drove from northern Maine into Canada, crossing the bridge to Prince Edward Island, birthplace and home province of Lucy Maud Montgomery, author of the *Anne of Green Gables* stories. I had watched all the "Anne of Green Gables" movies many times, as well as read the timeless book that inspired the movies. Mom, too, had devoured Montgomery's novels.

After spending so many hours lost in that marvelous world created in Ms. Montgomery's fertile mind, I felt a connection with Anne–her independent spirit, her emotionally charged temper when standing up for her truths, her innate sense of the beauty of solitude. I just *had* to see Prince Edward Island. It was absolutely captivating, with miles of sand dunes, the smell of the sea, the special way the northern sunlight sparkled on the water, the clay-colored cliffs–I found everything to be so quiet, so pure. I felt as if I had been transported back to a time long ago.

For Patti and me, the journey was just as exciting as the destination. She, being the passionate lover of animals, never had a qualm about screeching on her brakes to stop for a rabbit, a squirrel, or something bigger. Whenever we encountered a moose standing in the middle of the highway, he would simply stare us down, and we would wait until he decided to mosey along.

To this day Patti and I can spend hours and hours on a road trip, never tiring of travelling, never tiring of one another; just simply being. Our friendship is the kind where words need not be exchanged, just as it always was with Karine and me.

I planned to major in music. After twelve years under the tutelage of Miss Maude, I dreamed of becoming a concert pianist. The music department offered students the opportunity to take private lessons for credit from a selection of piano teachers in the community. The teacher I found taught from home in a small adjacent town. The only piano teacher I had ever known was Miss Maude. I assumed my new teacher would be like her—a competent, trustworthy music authority.

I drove to his house one cold, dreary winter afternoon. A thick layer of snow coated the sidewalks and streets, with flurries filling the air. It was not the kind of day to be out and about, but I prided myself on being a responsible student who took my studies seriously. Despite the terrible driving conditions I reached the instructor's home on schedule, walked in, and began my piano lesson.

What happened that day shocked me more than anything I'd ever experienced in my young life. As I sat on the piano bench, concentrating fully on the challenging piece I was learning, the instructor's hand reached towards me. Noticing this movement through my side vision, I assumed he was going to point out something in the sheet music in front of me or perhaps correct my technique. I was completely mistaken. His hand touched me. He made an attempt to grope my thigh and fondle me. Immediately I stood up and backed away. My heart pounded madly in my chest as fear welled up in my throat. The music I'd been studying left from my mind immediately, replaced by one pervading thought: *I've got to get out of here!* In an instant I ran out the door and jumped into my car. With my heart still racing and tears trickling down my face, I glanced in my rearview mirror. There he stood at his doorway leering at me with an evil look in his eyes. I'd never in my life seen anyone appear more demonic than him. I sped down the icy road back towards campus.

Back in the safety of my dorm room, I lay down on my bed, tears rolling down my cheeks. I was alone; Patti probably was at the science lab. Struggling to catch my breath, I looked at my body and noticed that I had broken out into hives. When Patti returned and asked what was wrong, I couldn't bring myself to tell her.

The next day I went to the Dean and simply told him I wanted to take an "Incomplete" for the course. It did not occur to me to speak up about what had happened, as I had been raised in a family where certain things were left unspoken, in an era when sex crimes went largely unreported. I thought it best to keep my mouth shut about the entire issue. I never said a word to anyone.

I don't know what happened to that music teacher. All I know is that I never saw him again, but the effects of his selfish, depraved act lingered on. In an instant he took away the love of piano Miss Maude had so carefully instilled in me throughout my youth. For years I avoided the piano. If someone asked me why I wasn't playing any longer, I simply said I had lost interest. Every time I tried to play the piano, his ominous face would appear in my mind, that satanic look haunting me, and I couldn't do it. Isn't it astonishing how one person, one incident, one moment, one second in a lifetime, really, can alter our lives so drastically? Or even that we allow it to affect us so deeply?

In retrospect, I would not have become a concert pianist even if this incident hadn't occurred. Despite twelve years of lessons with Miss Maude and a long-held desire to make a career out of my music, I don't have the discipline required of a successful concert pianist. But that is beside the point. That man had no right to assault me. How many others had he sexually abused? His depravity had a profoundly negative effect on me, especially during a time when I was seeking out who I was. Music would have continued to be prominent in my life had he not tarnished its beauty for me.

Fortunately, time can and does heal emotional wounds. I started lessons again in the spring of 2009. My teacher is Marie, pianist for a renowned orchestra in Southern California. She is such a blessing in my life. Her presence has ignited my musical spirit again. I am free of the burden from so many years ago. Today, nearly forty years later, I am back to playing the piano and loving it. I feel as if I have recaptured a vital part of my soul!

"As an eagle towards the sky." This was my college's motto.

At times, I felt just like that eagle, wings outstretched, flying boldly across the clear blue sky. Other times, I found myself plummeting down, spiraling out of control and plunging into the choppy Atlantic waters.

What kept me going during the challenging times? Letters from Karine. Though we were miles apart and I longed to be held in her arms, her presence was always with me. Opening her birthday cards and Christmas greetings was like releasing a breath of fresh air into my college life. I was comforted and thrilled by her cards. Every time I read one of her notes, I could hear her genuine laughter, see her gentle eyes, feel her strong arms around me. At least for a moment, everything was right with the world again.

My college years passed quickly. After graduating, I stepped into the great big world uncertain of what to do next. I had finished four years of a liberal arts education. By then, Dad had hired both Will and Matt, giving them key positions in his auto business. Their careers were taking off. With college degree in hand and the same level of education my brothers had received, I could have followed in their footsteps.

But it never would have occurred to Dad to ask me to go into business with them. In my part of the world, at that time, very few fathers would have asked a daughter to join the family business. That was a man's world. In my family, the topic of a career for me wasn't discussed. Instead of tackling the career issue head-on, I did what was expected of me. I got married.

CHAPTER FIVE

TRYING TO FIND
MY PLACE

Growing up, I always carried this insecurity that I was never good enough for Dad. It seemed to me that in his eyes, I simply wasn't smart enough or pretty enough. My feelings of inadequacy ran high around Mom as well. Appearance was of great importance to Mom, so she dressed me in fashionable clothes and taught me the latest make-up techniques.

With Mom constantly working to improve my physical appearance, and Dad always trying to elevate my intellect, I found it difficult to know who I really was. It was even harder for me to decide who I wanted to become. This insecurity affected my psyche and, at times, even my physical health. As a little girl, I frequently ended up at the doctor's office because of anxiety. I would complain about stomachaches or breathing problems, but the doctors could never find anything wrong. Regardless, these symptoms were real. I felt them, I feared them, and they got in the way of my enjoyment of life.

Some days my parents were at their wits' end trying to figure out what to do with me. All they needed to do, really, was simply leave me in Karine's care. Whenever I was with her, I was fine. No stomachaches. No breathing issues. I never felt anxious in Karine's presence. From my childhood into my teenage years, she simply loved me, and that unspoken, unconditional love served as a healing balm that calmed my nerves and dissolved any symptoms of anxiety. Nothing the doctors ever prescribed could do that.

With Karine, I always saw things clearly. I could be myself knowing that she would love and accept me no matter what. With everyone else, life was confusing. When I went away to college, I felt even more perplexed since the unlimited options to fully express myself were overwhelming to the sheltered Southern girl I was. Like a kid in a candy store, I wanted to try so many different kinds of music and clothing available to me. I changed my wardrobe to try to fit in with the exciting new college world that surrounded me.

When I came home during spring break my freshman year, I was dressed in a pair of jeans from L.L. Bean, certainly not a style I had ever worn before. In addition, I had put on what is commonly known as the "freshman fifteen," the dreaded fifteen pounds some female college students gain their first year away from home. I suppose I can attribute that weight gain to cafeteria cuisine and late-night runs to Dunkin' Donuts!

The moment Mom laid eyes on me she was horrified. What had happened to her little Southern girl? Patti was with me, and she still remembers how Mom lectured me about my appearance. Come Sunday, all of us went to Grandmother's house for the afternoon and for supper. We walked into her living room and, as always, found Grandmother sitting on her satin-covered sofa.

Immediately she shot me a suspicious look. "Bethany Ann, come here and let me take a look at you," she commanded.

I hesitated before taking a step toward her.

Grandmother looked me up and down, the disapproval on her face quickly escalating.

"Turn around, dear," she said.

I did as I was told, bracing myself for one of any number of insults that would surely materialize.

After several moments of strained silence, Grandmother merely stated, "You have put on quite a bit of weight."

"Yes Ma'am," I replied, quietly hoping that the scrutiny would end.

Mom and Dad stood back, looking on. They said nothing, but their troubled expressions spoke volumes. For the rest of the afternoon, I sat in silence in a chair in the corner of the living room desperately wishing I could disappear.

Why had I even gone home? Did I really need this kind of treatment? It was becoming more and more difficult to relate to Mom and Dad, to Grandmother, to the whole way of doing things in the South. If it wasn't for Karine, I might have packed up and left after being scolded and humiliated by my family.

I walked into the kitchen where Karine was busily preparing a meal. Hot tears burned in my eyes. She took one look at me and stopped what she was doing. With concern written across her face, she asked, "What's wrong, honey child?"

I told her everything. Through the tears I expressed my frustration and my pain. I shared what Mom had said to me and how upset she was about my weight gain. Karine's eyes filled with compassion. I could tell she wanted to say something to me, something important. She wanted to say it so badly, but she couldn't. In those days, an employee never spoke against her employer, especially not a black maid against her white boss. So she refrained from saying what was really on her mind.

Instead, she simply gave me one of her signature hugs that never failed to comfort and said, "Now don't you worry about that. I just think your mom is going through a lot with all you children gone." And that was that. Whenever she hugged me, I felt safe. At least for the moment, all was right again.

When I came home for summer break, Mom sent me halfway across the country to a spa in Southern California for two weeks to lose that dreaded "freshman fifteen." I got the message loud and clear. When I went back to college in the fall, I religiously watched everything I ate.

Before long I developed an obsessive personality. Throughout my twenties, I was absolutely obsessed with running. I *had* to run ten miles every day. There were no ifs, ands, or buts about it—I just had to do it. On top of that, I would binge eat. I never threw up, but I wasn't afraid to take laxatives. Every day I took a long, hard look at myself in the mirror, but the image staring back at me was never good enough. I'd proceed to spend the rest of the day straining to be perfect, hoping that I would find something better the next morning when I looked into the mirror again.

I never did. My mind was caught in a vicious circle, always ending up at the same point. Always unimpressed with who I was or how I looked. Always yearning to be someone I wasn't.

Throughout my teen years, Mom loved to take me clothes shopping. We shopped at the primo stylish boutique for teenage girls where Mom always picked what she wanted me to wear. In the eyes of the girls at my school, I was someone who had it together: Surely my beautiful outfits matched the self-confidence that lived inside. How wrong they were. Little did anyone know that underneath that picture-perfect surface I was riddled with insecurity.

I dressed for Mom. Even today there are times when I buy an outfit and there is that small voice in my head asking the age-old question …

"Would Mom approve?"

I felt pulled and prodded in every direction. Dad expected nothing less than perfection in my academic endeavors. Mom expected nothing less than physical flawlessness. Southern girls in my world were expected to be debutantes, a rite of passage required of every proper young lady in Memphis. It may have been expected of me, but there was no way I was going to take part in this Southern belle tradition. It simply wasn't me.

Grandmother was absolutely mortified. What an embarrassment that her own granddaughter refused to be properly introduced to high society! But Mom knew I could not be challenged on this one. She did not even ask why. I believe that in her heart of hearts, she knew why, and in her own way, she supported me. Even though appearances mattered to her, she knew that I disliked the stigma and pretense associated with being a debutante. I'm certain that she herself didn't much care for it, either.

Deep down inside, underneath the polished outfits and classic, elegant look she worked so hard to cultivate, Mom was a simple country girl. In my opinion, she felt she had to be someone that Memphis society expected her to be. For whatever reason, she had a profound need to fit in and have her only daughter look the part, too.

After Savannah was born Mom was not happy about the way I dressed my little girl. But I had very different goals; I wanted Savannah to be an independent child with her own voice. Growing up, my daughter had a strong, outgoing personality. She was a little tomboy and her world revolved around horses, so I didn't bother to dress her in fancy smocked dresses except for on holidays and special occasions. The rest of the time, Savannah needed practical clothes. Though I stuck to my instincts, deep down I knew that once again I was disappointing Mom. Once again, I just wasn't good enough.

As a college sophomore, when I headed home during one of my breaks, I could not wait to see Karine and feel her warm embrace! It would be just like old times. We'd watch TV together, she'd bake me chocolate chip cookies, we'd laugh about the funny things in life, and her hugs would make me feel safe.

But it was not to be. Mom broke the news to me— Karine had left. She had accepted a job elsewhere, taking care of another little girl. This news caught me completely by surprise. I'd grown up with Karine; she was *family. More than family.* She was my spiritual teacher, the one person who accepted and loved me unconditionally. And now, she was gone. I felt devastated. I guess I just assumed she'd always be there, waiting for me with open arms. The thought of her taking care of another little girl was almost too much to bear. I was so envious and heartbroken!

I was dealing with shock, loss, and grief, but this time, there was no one to share my feelings with, nobody to comfort me. Karine had been the one and only person I could share with completely. The house felt cold and empty without her. I could not imagine the rest of my life without her any more than I could imagine Memphis without the Mississippi River flowing protectively alongside.

Then one day, I got a wonderful surprise: Karine came by our home to visit me. I was so excited I ran out to the car, only to find a cute little girl sitting in the passenger seat. Oh how my heart dropped. But I kept a smile on my face. I ran around to Karine's side of the car. As soon as she opened the door I leaned in and gave her a big hug. She held me so tightly.

"Oh honey," she said in her sweet, motherly way, "it's so good to see you. So all grown up!" Tears welled in my eyes, but I didn't care. The little girl sat so sweetly and looked on. I smiled back. Life goes on. Naturally it was time for Karine to move on and take care of another child as lovingly as she'd taken care of me. But forever in my mind, I am Karine's little girl.

After raising Will, Matt and me in Memphis, and after we had left the nest, Mom and Dad decided it was time to head west. Perhaps they could not bear to live in a huge empty house, alone and isolated from the world. Needing a fresh start, they ended up where Mom had refused to raise her family: Southern California. Times had changed, circumstances were different, and the West Coast seemed the right choice at that point in their lives. They moved during my sophomore year. The move did not happen overnight, though. It was a progression of sorts.

Mom and Dad had begun to think about selling our home and moving into a townhome when I was still a college freshman. When I went home for the summer after my first year of college, the late soul singer-songwriter Hayes Harper came by one afternoon to take a look at our house, which had been put on the market.

After winning a Grammy Award, Mr. Harper had become an international star. I vividly remember the day he visited our home; it was an absolute honor to meet him. Despite his celebrity status, he was such a kind, gentle man. His soft-spoken and humble ways endeared him to everyone. When he walked into our living room and saw the grand piano in the corner, his entire body perked up.

"Who plays?" he asked.

I took a tiny step forward and softly replied, "I do. I play classical music."

Without a word, Mr. Harper took a seat at the piano and looked at me, flashing a huge, warm grin.

"Would you play something for me?" he asked.

I froze, every muscle in my body tightening up. Isaac Hayes was asking me to play the piano for him? I was mortified.

Sensing my fear, he took a look at the notes of the Beethoven sonata I was currently practicing. After a few seconds he simply and humbly said, "I don't know how to read music. Please, play a little."

A smile broke out across my face. Though I was completely terrified, I felt so honored to be asked. So I did it. I played the piano for Harper Hayes. Can you believe it? After I was finished, he kindly thanked and praised me. Speechless, all I could do was muster a shy grin.

Dad took Mr. Harper outside to see the vegetable garden. Growing up, Mr. Harper had picked cotton in Tennessee, so I am quite certain he knew much more about the ways of gardening than Dad did!

Come November of 1973, Mr. Harper bought our home. Mom and Dad downsized to a lovely townhome in Memphis before moving permanently to Southern California. This transaction did not go unnoticed in our still segregated part of the world. Though a celebrity and a talented musician, Mr. Harper was a black man moving into an upper middle class white neighborhood, and that raised more than a few eyebrows.

A November 1973 article in the morning Memphis newspaper stated that Mr. Harper had purchased our home. The piece said that Dad "... declined knowledge of the purchaser's identity ... he refused to allow a photographer to take pictures of the house today ..."

The evening newspaper ran an article the following day that tour family was "... scheduled to move out tomorrow and that a 24-hour guard will be posted on the property ..."

The city buzzed with gossip. But Dad didn't care. He never cared what people thought of him. He liked and admired Mr. Harper, and he was thrilled to have our beautiful home end up in such good hands.

Months later I heard that Mr. Harper had transformed Will's and Matt's bedrooms into His and Her Salons! I would like to have seen that.

And do you know that eventually Mr. Harper sold our home to a Jewish synagogue? For many years our house served as a synagogue. While visiting Memphis one year, Matt decided to go to our old property to have a look around. A rabbi came up to him.

"Can I help you with something?"

"No, thank you. I'm just looking around. I used to live here."

"Well, you must be from the automobile family because you certainly aren't black!"

In time our house was torn down and a real synagogue was built in its place. But the marks of my childhood are still there—the woods, the scents, and the boulders Dad had placed randomly around the property ... memories everywhere.

It didn't take Mom and Dad long to figure out they did not like living in their Memphis townhome. It simply didn't fit their style. After a brief period there, Dad decided it was time to move to a town by the ocean in Southern California, a part of the world he had always loved. After he and Mom moved in 1974, his goal was to retire, to settle down completely. But he quickly realized that he couldn't ignore that itch to work again. He bought a small Mercedes-Benz/Oldsmobile dealership, which over the years Will and Matt built into an auto empire still going strong today.

I can't help thinking how ironic it is that Mom and Dad ended up in exactly the place where they didn't want to raise their kids—Southern California, home of Hollywood and land of the Beach Boys. My parents were happy with their move, but I wasn't so sure I'd like it. Going home during breaks suddenly meant heading to the West Coast instead of going to the South. Wasn't it ironic that after wanting desperately to leave the South as a high school student, I found myself not ready to let go of my riverside roots?

Despite California's natural beauty and days of sunshine, I had a difficult time fitting in. Seasons felt boring to me; all of them blended into a perpetual spring. Weather-wise there was little difference between Christmas and the Fourth of July. I missed the Memphis markers that signaled a distinct transition from one time of year to the next.

My parents' new home was lovely, though. This is where I stayed whenever I had a break from college. Set atop a hillside overlooking the Pacific Ocean, the house was a smaller version of the home I grew up in. My bedroom walls were pale yellow, and the floral bedspreads matched perfectly. When I first stepped in, I immediately felt a wave of warmth and comfort. Though it was not the room I had left back in Memphis, it was designed in a way that felt familiar. It felt good to me, comfortable. As I looked around, though, I noticed something important was missing.

I walked out of my new bedroom. "Mom!"

"What is it, honey?"

"What happened to my stuffed animals?"

"We had to throw those out, dear. There were soot problems in the old home. All your animals were ruined."

Getting rid of my stuffed animal collection may have been the practical thing to do, but I felt such anguish in my chest. Why hadn't anyone told me that my treasures were being thrown away? I could have driven down from college one weekend to salvage my favorites. I opened my mouth to complain, but something stopped me. Suddenly I felt silly and overly sentimental. Of what use were ancient stuffed animals to me as a 20-year-old?

It didn't take me long to realize that it wasn't so much the missing stuffed animals that upset me, it was what they symbolized. Their absence reflected the end of an era. I wasn't a kid anymore. My childhood home was gone, my childhood toys were gone, and most painful of all, my best friend Karine was gone from my life. Where was that sweet presence that had brightened up every room, those strong arms that had held me so close and made me feel safe?

It took longer to realize that Karine hadn't really left me. I still was, and always would be, her "special little girl." Even though the world I'd grown up in was tucked away neatly in the past, and my future was yet to be determined, Karine lived on in my broken open heart. Though miles away and worlds apart, we still shared a special bond. Karine has never left my side ...

I won't deny it—the Golden State took some getting used to. My first summer in Southern California was lonely and, quite frankly, miserable! My best friends from Memphis had stayed in the South, and Patti lived in Maine. So I spent that entire summer alone, for the most part. While the young people around me were enjoying the surf and sun, wishing that each summer day would go on forever, I wished for just the opposite. I wanted to get back to college. Being in Southern California made me feel like a fish out of water, and every day I longed to be tossed back into the ocean.

With summer finally over, I flew back to Maine, relieved to get back to what I knew. I felt I was home again. It was now my junior year.

***

The seventeenth-century French theologian Bossuet once wrote, "The heart has reasons that reason does not understand," a sentiment mirrored by seventeenth-century philosopher and mathematics genius Pascal who wrote, "The heart has its reasons which reason knows nothing of." This I know to be true. While some people find that special someone seemingly without effort and spend a lifetime together, others (like me) experience chapters of love instead.

It was great to be back in school, back in Maine, and back with my special friend Sean, an adorable Boston Irish Catholic hockey star with piercing blue eyes and jet-black hair. We had met early on freshman year in the cafeteria. Patti and I were eating lunch. As I looked around my eyes locked with his. He gave me a wink, which was quite unsettling. I took my tray to the kitchen and felt a presence right behind me. I slowly turned around to find him, lunch tray in hand, staring at me. "What are you doing?" I asked. "I don't know", he responded. And that was that ... several weeks later we ran into each other on campus, and thus began a beautiful friendship.

Junior year began with all of our usual fun times. I attended his hockey practices and games, cheering with gusto as his number one fan. We spent hours together doing homework while listening to our favorite band, "America". Whenever I looked up and saw Sean's deep blue eyes smiling back at me, my heart warmed. In his presence I felt safe and at peace.

During those times when we walked together to classes or saw each other on weekends, we would lose ourselves in conversation. It didn't matter what we talked about; we were so comfortable, so at home with each other. And yet, we were too close to go out on a real date. Maybe we just didn't want to ruin our friendship by telling one another our true feelings. So I dated others, and Sean continued to see his high school sweetheart whenever he went home to Boston. If only one of us had the guts to confide in the other and say out loud what we both felt in our hearts, things might have worked out differently...

The saddest day of my college life came when Sean shared startling news. "I'm married now," he told me. For a moment I couldn't breathe. This was so unexpected!

His girlfriend was pregnant. His upbringing and sense of duty told him that marrying her was the right thing to do. I didn't disagree with him, but I felt that love was missing from the equation. How could a marriage built upon obligation stand the test of time? Nevertheless, my Southern upbringing had taught me how to put on a smile and save face even when my heart was breaking. So that is exactly what I did.

"Still friends?" he asked.

"Sure", I responded.

I knew I now had to "bury" Sean. My dear friend was now a married man. Campus life was never the same again. If only...

Paul came into my life in January of 1976—my senior year, Paul's junior year. We were in the same archaeology class. Truth be told, I really wasn't interested in pursuing a relationship. It was my last semester of college, and I just wanted to focus on my studies and graduate.

But when Paul and I met, we definitely felt chemistry between us. We became friends instantly. Without a doubt, we shared a certain bond. Paul knew how to make me laugh, which was exactly what I needed in my life at the time. He asked me out, and we dated for the rest of the semester.

After I graduated that spring of '76 with a B.A. in Art History, I flew back to Southern California, back to Mom and Dad. I was 22 and had absolutely no idea what I wanted to do with my life. Dad was satisfied I had my college degree. I had accomplished what he wanted: I had attained an excellent education. But I knew I wanted more ... even though I didn't exactly know what *more* was. Mom and Dad couldn't understand this. We were living in the 1970s, a time when girls were burning their bras and pursuing their own careers. But such actions were millions of miles away from Mom and Dad's world.

That summer Paul and I kept in contact. Trying to find some kind of purpose in my life, I got a job as a bank teller. However, I still wasn't enjoying Southern California. Without telling Mom and Dad, I applied for a temporary position in the Alumni Office at a preparatory girls' school outside of Boston. I said absolutely nothing about this until a job offer actually came in. Only then did I tell Mom and Dad. They showed no signs of approval or disapproval, so in September I left California and headed back to New England.

Most weekends I commuted to my old school to visit Paul. He lived in the condos by the soccer field. On a dreary spring afternoon, we were hanging out in the living area of his place. He made us both a cup of tea. Just before I was about to take my last sip, I noticed a diamond ring at the bottom of the cup. I paused, looked up at him, and looked back at the ring.

"Will you marry me?" Paul asked.

I simply answered, "Yeah, sure."

And that was that.

We decided to get married that August of '77 in Southern California. After he graduated we hopped in his car and headed to the West Coast. During our cross-country drive we dreamed about possibilities for our future, maybe living in Colorado with Paul working as a ski instructor and me working the desk position at a ski resort. I couldn't help but feel attracted to the refreshing zest for adventure that Paul exhibited. I had never known anyone quite like him, and I so much wanted to carve out an exciting journey together with this man.

We never did go to Colorado. Soon after we married Dad asked Paul if he would be interested in working at the dealership. Thinking it would be a great opportunity, Paul accepted. The wild adventures we had envisioned never came to fruition. In fact, they completely died the day that Paul agreed to start working for Dad.

Paul and I played the roles of husband and wife; he was the provider, I was the homemaker. For a long time, we played our parts to perfection, letting go of our desire to take chances, to move boldly ahead, to know ourselves. For once in my life, I was actually fitting the mold. And I was doing it rather flawlessly.

I believe that every relationship serves a purpose, and the greater purpose of our relationship was to bring into the world two precious children. Savannah was born in 1981 and Steven arrived in 1984. My husband's and my roles really started to take dimension. Savannah and

Steven were shining lights across the field of my discontent. They filled me with such purpose, such compassion, such love. Being parents meant the world to Paul and me. It changed everything for us. Suddenly, we had a foundation; our marriage had a foundation. Our relationship together was built around our kids.

But we never grew together as a couple. I can honestly say now that at that time, Paul and I were simply not mature enough to make things work between us. We were young and emotionally unprepared for marriage. We did not have the strong core that was needed for a healthy marriage. Despite years of counseling and Bible studies, nothing could save our relationship.

We simply grew apart.

CHAPTER SIX

IN MEMORY OF MOM

Writing about Mom is difficult. It's hard to think back and remember who she was, exactly, during my youth. The Lord took her when I was thirty-six. Somehow I felt robbed that she and I never had the opportunity to truly know one another, to be friends as adults, to embrace and enjoy Savannah and Stephen together, to grow older and older together. I struggle to express how I truly feel because, honestly, I still don't know. But I do know this with certainty: The day Mom died marked the beginning of a downward spiral for me that, if grace had not intervened, would have ended my life prematurely.

There was much to admire about Mom. She was so beautiful and gracious, and had the most gorgeous, radiant smile and irresistible dimples. But I felt that smile was a façade for the world; it did not reflect how she really felt inside. I would often find Mom sitting in her bedroom suite, alone, with tears in her eyes. The beauty in her face looked as if it had been crushed, weighed down by things beyond her control. Whenever I asked what was wrong, she wiped away her tears and simply replied, "Oh nothing, honey."

As a teenager, I did not know how to respond. Not knowing what to do or how to help, I immersed myself in my own activities. Now I find myself looking back and wondering *Who was she? What was she crying about? Where did her pain come from?*

I get the sense that she felt like a misfit. Did she feel she was living in a world that really wasn't for her? What was missing from her life? Had her dreams slipped through her fingers? Although in the world's eyes Mom seemingly had it all, it was obvious from the tears she tried to hide, and from many other signs, that she was not happy. During her last few years she appeared to have given up on life. In some ways, I had become an outsider. I felt Mom slipping away, disconnecting from the world, yet I felt powerless to help her. I wish I had been able to get inside her mind and soul, to know her thoughts ... to know her.

Near the end of her life, Mom had an operation to remove a tumor from her adrenal gland. Though the tumor was removed, her doctor remained cautious. "There's still a possibility the cancer has spread," he told us, avoiding eye contact. "We'll have to wait and see."

I believe Dad knew she was not going to live much longer, but he wasn't quite ready to let go. Wanting to make more memories with his life partner, he chartered a glorious yacht for cruising in the Bahamas. He knew this would be their last trip together to this place, to these waters they so dearly loved. Savannah, Steven, and I were able to join them on this final voyage.

By the time we left for our trip, Mom had become so thin. She had lost her appetite and refused to eat anything we put in front of her. Dad hoped the trip would bring back her spark. It didn't. She grew weaker and weaker.

Whenever I found Dad sitting in a chair on that yacht looking across the beautiful Bahamian waters, his eyes full of tears, I sat quietly next to him. I didn't have to say a word. In silence we worried about Mom and grieved over her rapidly declining health. I simply hoped my presence during those moments was enough to give Dad some measure of comfort.

When Mom became so ill that she began throwing up blood, Dad cut the trip short and made arrangements for a plane to pick them up from one of the islands. Back in Southern California, he checked her directly into a hospital. There we officially learned that our worst nightmare had become reality: Mom's cancer had spread throughout her body. Mom chose not to do chemo or radiation, as the doctors said treatment would simply prolong the inevitable.

Dad took her home so she could live out her last days in the home she loved so that beautiful Mediterranean-style villa overlooking the Pacific from atop a hill. Mom's bedroom was fit for a queen, decorated in white and cream with floor-to-ceiling windows facing the ocean. Photos of her children and grandchildren filled the walls.

She was leaving us at such a quick pace. The cancer progressed rapidly, ultimately spreading into her brain. Week after week I spent days by her side. Few words were spoken for she no longer had the strength.

The morning she died, I somehow knew this would be the day. It was Dad's 62nd birthday. I sat next to Mom on her bed holding her hand. As I glanced at the family pictures on the walls, I spotted a photo of me as a freckle faced ten-year-old looking sheepishly at the camera, dressed in a simple, tasteful blue and white sleeveless dress. I asked Mom if she knew that little girl. In response, she squeezed my hand. Warmth filled me, and I began to cry quietly. Mom did not have the strength to say the words, but that squeeze communicated her message loud and clear: *I love you.*

I arranged the soft silk sheets carefully around her frail body, trying to keep her comfortable. As I gently rested my head on her chest, tears continued to quietly roll down my cheeks. Within moments, Mom took her final breath. I lifted my head and looked at her face. Truly, her countenance had a smile. I knew without a doubt that Mom had entered those beautiful pearly gates Karine had talked about so long ago. A quiet peace filled the bedroom.

I let go of her hand and walked down the long travertine hallway to the den. Dad, sitting in his chair staring out the window at the endless Pacific, was lost in his thoughts. The ocean was tranquil, not one ripple to be found. Overcome with heartache, Dad simply couldn't bear to be in the room with Mom that morning. His wife of forty years had quietly slipped out of his life.

I looked into my father's eyes and said, "Dad, it's time to come to the bedroom."

His shoulders caved in, his lips quivered. He knew exactly what my words meant. He nodded and got up from his chair, following me to the bedroom where Mom lay so eerily still. Dad took one look at her and fell to his knees sobbing, "Oh Jo Ann, why you and not me?"

Numbness overtaking me, I called Will and Matt at work. Both arrived within minutes. Will mourned quietly while Matt, like Dad, fell on his knees and wept. For some reason I felt like an observer, as though I was standing as a witness behind a thick sheet of glass. I wept the hardest for Matt. He and Mom had always had such a special bond.

The morning Mom died was another glorious, sunny Southern California day. What a stark contrast to the grief so pronouncedly felt within these bedroom walls. How difficult to perceive that beyond those walls life was going on ... simply another day.

The morticians came to wrap Mom and take her away. One of them was a large, strong black man with the gentlest face. He looked at me with a deep knowing that was familiar and cryptic all at once. I looked deeply into his eyes and warmth filled my soul, that same warmth I had felt every time Karine had looked into my eyes. I could have sworn those were her eyes. How thankful I was that she had found a way to bring me comfort when I needed it most.

Little did I know at the time that I would see this gentleman again in another ten years, and again in another three years following. Yes, the same gentle giant with large, soulful eyes wrapped and rolled away three people I dearly loved.

How brief life is.

The night of Mom's death was the beginning of my demise. With Paul by my side, I sat in silence sipping a glass of wine. That one glass of wine turned into countless more over the next seven years. That's the thing about funny breath—it can happen in an instant before you know what has hit you. It is cunning, insidious.

Mom passed away at the age of 63. If she were alive today, she'd be in her late eighties. Sometimes I try to see her face in my mind, but it's difficult to picture her. I keep a photo of her in my entranceway as a continual reminder of her presence. I focus on the beautiful memories, the qualities that made her special—her beauty, her grace, her class, her goodness.

CHAPTER SEVEN

FINDING MOM,
FINDING MYSELF

One morning, I awoke with a deep longing in my chest. It was a longing to find and reclaim Mom. I had lost her in her later years when life had trampled the spirit of this amazing woman Obviously I couldn't reclaim her in the physical sense, but I knew there was another way to get close to Mom. My plan was to seek out her roots, her home. In the fall of 2008, I took a trip to the heart of Tennessee.

The day I arrived in her home town was cold and dreary, yet the autumn leaves glistened in vivid color as if protesting against the thick glumness that hung over the countryside. My journey began. I drove into town, eagerly looking out the window, trying to store every detail in my mind. The simple, tiny town square was exactly as I had remembered it. A few people strolled along the streets, walking leisurely as if they had all the time in the world. I continued down the avenue where Miss Macy's and the bustling hotel had once stood. Though new homes took their places, I could almost smell that fried chicken in the dining room at the hotel. I could almost see that small, stark guest room at Miss Macy's where Papa lived before he met Miss Ruth.

Most of the buildings in the town square had been renovated into new stores. Rexall Drugs and the Princess Theater were the only two places that remained from when Mom lived here. I smiled as I drove by Rexall, remembering those cherry colas I so enjoyed as a kid. Oh, I can still taste them!

I drove down the "old road," now a highway, and was surprised to see a new brick house standing where Great-Grandmother Ida's whiteboard house used to be. The outhouse still remained in the backyard, though. Across the highway was empty land where the cotton gin once stood. Across the road, an empty lot had replaced the general store. It all resonated strongly with me, bringing me back to many years before. In my mind, I saw Will, Matt, and me running to the general store to get a Coca-Cola from the chest and maybe a few gum balls. I even saw the locals sitting in their wooden chairs, chatting about the latest news in town. It all came flooding back.

I ventured on to drive by the home where Papa and Miss Ruth had lived, a simple wooden house sitting on a hill along the main road. As I looked at the house I remembered the delicious Southern fare Miss Ruth prepared, especially her strawberry cakes. From my purse I pulled out a black-and-white photo of this special couple taken on my grandfather's last day as a mail carrier after 45 years of service. The year was 1966. Love for Papa coursed through me as I admired the photo. I marveled at the dramatic changes he must have seen delivering mail across five decades, first on a mule, then with a horse and buggy, and finally driving a Chevy!

I continued along the road, stopping at a general store across the street from where Papa and Miss Ruth had lived. The two women who ran the store had been old high school classmates of Mom's. When I walked in, I found them sitting with a group of men. Everyone was sipping coffee and smoking cigarettes, chatting away about matters of the day. It was as if time stood still.

As soon as the group saw me, the store fell silent. I walked toward everybody and politely introduced myself as Jo Ann's daughter.

All of a sudden, bits of chatter filled the air once more.

"Oh yeah, we remember Jo Ann."

"You look just like her."

"Oh, and Harry! He was our postman."

"Do you know I still have one of those collars Ethel made?"

I couldn't get a word in edgewise. I was speechless listening to all of them talk about special people from my past. More forgotten memories came flooding back. I thought about Gramma Ethel and Mom, especially about how they took a risk and moved to Memphis together. While working at a jewelry store and the post office, Gramma Ethel started making women's collars on the side. It turned out she did pretty well with those collars—the department store J.C. Penny's bought many of them. I remembered sitting on a wooden stool in her factory when I was little, watching her make those pretty collars.

Bidding this lively group farewell, I left the general store and drove a few miles down the small country road from Great-Grandmother Ida's house. From the car I watched the beautiful countryside with its array of fall colors roll by my window. I'd never been to my next destination, since Mom had never taken us there when we visited Ida. As I drove along my stomach felt queasy, and when I arrived, I knew why.

I hesitantly got out of the car and began walking. I came upon a few worn-down buildings and the remains of an old train track covered in overgrown weeds. As I took in this broken town, my heart sank. I said to myself softly with tears welling in my eyes, "So this is Huron." I did not want to believe that this decaying, abandoned town had been such a big part of Mom's youth.

I remembered how Mom and Gramma Ethel had described it when I was a little girl. It had been a small town with its own postal office where Papa worked and a train depot where people caught the train to visit bigger towns. It had a dance hall where the whole town would gather on weekends to dance and bootleggers would be selling their whiskey. Those were the days of the Depression and World War II, and folks celebrated being alive. This was where Mom had learned to dance.

I could picture Mom with her dimples and beautiful smile dancing to "Boogie Woogie Bugle Boy" and "Chattanooga Choo Choo." She was such a graceful dance. Her dancing days had started right here in this small, humble town. I clearly remember Mom and Dad floating across the dance floor of the Plaza Hotel in New York City in 1964. With delicate, precise movements they made the ballroom dance look like a work of art. I was ten, and as I sat at the table holding the softest, fluffiest white stuffed bear Mom and Dad had bought me at the FAO Schwarz toy store, I stared at them in awe. They looked as if they had stepped straight out of a Fred Astaire and Ginger Rogers movie.

I returned to the car and sat in silence awhile as I processed everything I had seen. I bid a fond farewell to the past and drove back to Memphis. My life changed a bit after that day. I had found Mom. In doing so, I reclaimed an important part of myself.

CHAPTER EIGHT

DESCENT INTO ALCOHOLISM AND CHAOS

The year 1990 is forever engrained in my mind. It's the year that I lost Mom, and the year that Paul and I separated. It was all too much to bear. I withdrew from the world, turning to alcohol for escape, for comfort, for support. The only joy I experienced was with my children, Savannah and Steven. Thank God for them! They were, and always will be, rays of light in my life, a life that otherwise was marching steadily downhill that fateful year of loss.

Although I drank in college, I did not consider myself an alcoholic during those years. Like the rest of my friends, I drank only at weekend parties. Though I had the inevitable hangover, I didn't think much about it because so did everyone else I knew. It was socially accepted and expected as far as I could see.

After Mom died and Paul and I split up, though, I drank for very different reasons. There was nothing social about my drinking. I turned to alcohol to escape the world, not to experience it. Alcohol numbed the pain and quieted my anxiety. Little did I know that my growing penchant for "funny breath" would invade my life.

After Paul and I decided to separate, I wanted nothing more than to get out of Southern California. But the question was: Where would I go, exactly? Savannah was twelve and Steven was eight. I wanted my choice to benefit them as well. I started toying with the idea of going to graduate school. I already had a bachelor's degree in art history, but I knew that if I truly wanted to apply my education, I would have to get at least a Master of Arts.

Where though?

One day, the answer came to me clearly: Memphis. I would go back to my roots. Though the region and I had our differences, the mighty Mississippi was calling me back to my childhood home. There was something romantic about rediscovering the old amidst what was supposed to be a time of renewal, regeneration, and rebirth. It was like starting all over again, but with the comfort of familiarity to guide me through. Not only that, but my children would have the opportunity to understand more about who I was and where I came from.

The prospect of living in Memphis grew more and more appealing as the months went by. After learning about an M.A. program in art history at the University of Memphis, I decided to apply. First I took the

GRE, the standardized test required for graduate school admissions. Then I got on the phone and contacted two schools for my children. I called my former school to ask about enrolling Savannah, and I called another top-quality school to talk about enrolling Steven.

I was elated to learn that both schools would gladly accept my children into their programs! How exciting that they would get to experience the places of learning that had meant so much to Will, Matt, and me. My children would get to experience a new pocket of life, a look into our roots. They had lived in Southern California all their lives, and the novelty of Memphis was a great new chapter for them. Paul supported my decision, and he made plans to visit our kids every six weeks. During their vacations, Savannah, Steven, and I would return to California where they could stay with their dad. It seemed everything was working out perfectly for each of us.

I was accepted into the M.A. program at the University of Memphis. My children and I left for Memphis in January of 1993. They began their second semesters at their new schools, Savannah in sixth grade and Steven in second grade. That spring I worked as an intern with the Education Department at a local fine arts museum prior to starting school in the fall.

The city I had known so well in the sixties looked similar to the one I was familiarizing myself with in the nineties. I was excited about reconnecting with some of the girls I had grown up with. In my mind, the experience my kids and I had embarked upon was going to be fun and rewarding. For me, it would be about reconnecting with old friends and engaging in the adventure of graduate school. For Savannah and Steven, it would be about making new friends and experiencing life in the world their mom and uncles had grown up in. I was eager and optimistic. This fresh start gave me renewed energy and a hopeful attitude, two vital attributes I had recently abandoned due to the challenges in my life.

I did reconnect with a few of my friends who were still living in the area, but these reunions weren't quite what I had expected. I was naïve to think that time had stood still and relationships would remain the same. Though all were friendly, the twenty-plus years that had passed maintained a distance between us. Our paths had diverged; they had their lives, I had mine.

I thought about Karine often, wishing she could hold me in her arms. I thought about what life must have been like for her. As a child I hadn't thought anything of her struggles. What an amazing woman Karine was, always managing to keep a smile on her face no matter what others said or how much rejection she faced. She exuded happiness, a genuine, heartfelt joy that came from her faith and that inner strength she possessed. How I took it all for granted in my younger years! Looking back, I realized just how much Karine's indomitable presence and invincible spirit impacted my life, then and now.

The Memphis homecoming I was expecting never materialized. Instead, I felt like a stranger in a strange land. It was lonely, isolating. What's more, I was torn by guilt, wondering what I had done to my children. Seduced by the romantic notion of rediscovering my roots, I had uprooted Savannah and Steven from the life they knew in California for a dream that failed to take form. I had yanked them away from friends and family, from all that was familiar, and placed them in a culture that was foreign to them.

I learned a very important lesson from this episode in my life. I learned that "one can never go home again." Nothing stands still. Lives move forward. Changes happen. What we once knew as "home" lives on only in our memories and heart.

I did an awful lot of soul-searching trying to figure out my next steps. I could drop everything and head back to California with Savannah and Steven. But that didn't feel right. I'd been accepted into graduate school. I had to complete the program. Besides, my father didn't raise his daughter to be a quitter. In my heart I felt deeply that I'd be failing Dad if I quit the program. And I'd be failing myself.

My course of action was to work as hard as I could for the next two years to complete the required coursework in Memphis. As soon as that was done, Savannah, Steven, and I would move back to Southern California where they could resume their lives in the schools they had attended, with the friends they'd been close to, and I would write my final thesis by correspondence. It wasn't perfect, but it was a workable solution.

God always seems to find a way to bring angels into our lives during the toughest of times. (And mind you, angels appear in many different guises!) For me during my challenging time in Memphis, that angel was Hollye.

I'll never forget the day I met her, my very first day of grad school. I was sitting quietly in the front row of my first class of the day—nineteenth-century European art. Class was just about to begin when this petite red-head, dressed in black from head to toe, plopped herself in the seat next to me.

She looked over and exclaimed, "Would you quit talking so much!"

Startled, I simply looked back at her, not knowing how to respond.

But she let me off the hook within a few seconds by cracking a smile and sticking her hand out.

"Hi, I'm Hollye." Thus began our friendship. Without it, I don't know if I could have seen graduate school through to the end.

Hollye is nine years my junior, and she came to Memphis from Georgia. I had never met a Southern girl quite like her. She was a far left-wing liberal, the complete opposite of the conservative family I'd grown up with. With her witty sarcasm that bordered on causticity and her devotion to veganism, Hollye definitely did not fit the profile of the Southern belles I had known throughout my childhood.

She rented a one-bedroom attic in a house one mile from campus. With her full-time scholarship, Hollye was on a mission. Every cell in her body was filled with determination. Nothing and no one was going to get in the way of her graduating. She completed the master's program in two years and then headed off to the Northwest to begin a new life as an artist.

Hollye was a wonderful distraction. She did not care what people thought of her. She was who she was—that simple. On occasion she would even show up to class in her pajamas! I think it was her way of telling the professors she was always in overload! Hollye had a heart of pure gold underneath that caustic, sometimes crude, exterior. She was a genuine friend to me, and she taught me to not take myself so seriously.

During school vacations Savannah, Steven, and I went home to California to spend time with family and friends. I never mentioned my loneliness in Memphis, and I certainly did not mention my drinking, which had been escalating. I was still fooling myself into believing I didn't have a problem. During the daytime hours I was highly functioning (at least I believed myself to be). I thought I had things under control.

After I completed two years of graduate school, the children and I said goodbye to Memphis. We finally made our way back home to California, for good. I spent the next two years working on my thesis by correspondence. Savannah, Steven, and I were so happy to be back. But there was one thing that followed me home... funny breath.

I realized that as much as I leaned on Karine's spirit for strength, I did not have her fortitude. I could not stop drinking.

"It was only wine, so it's not a big deal."

That's often one of the excuses that alcoholics use. I clung to that excuse as if my life depended on it. Wrapped in a coat of denial, I went about my business, intent upon proving to myself that I had everything under control.

Somewhere between 1995 and 1997, Savannah and Steven began realizing that something wasn't right with me. During the evenings, while they did their homework, they noticed that I would sit at the kitchen table and hide my wine under my chair. Every now and then, when I thought they weren't looking, I would take a quick sip.

There were even times that I got behind the driver's wheel when I had no business doing so. Though I'm not proud to admit this, I actually drove Savannah and Steven while intoxicated. My mind was painted thick with denial. I continued to let myself believe that everything was okay.

Once, I picked Steven up from the library and started driving home. I had been drinking earlier, so my reflexes were slow. I hit the curb, causing one of the tires to go flat. Without hesitating, Steven jumped out of the car and ran away from me. I sprang out of the car and chased after him. "Steven, please come back," I pleaded.

He turned to look at me, as if expecting more words.

But I didn't know what else to say.

His eyes filled with tears. "Mom, please don't do this."

His words broke my heart. They tore into me like a knife. I finally started to realize something I should have seen long ago: I needed help.

We got home and I went to my bedroom, the new realization sitting like lead in the pit of my stomach. I thought about Mom and how different she would get when she drank. I thought about Gramma Ethel and the black eyes she'd get, the blood on her gown from falling in a drunken stupor and hurting herself, and how alcohol had taken so much from her.

That's when I realized there was a pattern.

Up until that point, I never really considered that I had an alcohol issue. I started to look back at the times when I drank. Each and every time, I realized, I allowed myself to have too much. I went to bed crying. I knew I needed help.

I racked my brain for options. Who could I turn to?

I worried about Savannah and Steven. How would I be able to get through this and take care of them at the same time? I considered going to Dad for help, but immediately pushed the thought from my mind. He was a big drinker himself. How could he possibly help me with this problem?

I'd hit a dead end. Too embarrassed to ask anyone for help, I continued with the drinking. Every night I drank one or two bottles of wine down to the last drop.

Day after day I continued this way, ensnared by the false comfort of alcohol, for another whole year.

And then, in April of 1997, everything shifted dramatically.

For my 43rd birthday, my family took me out to dinner to one of the finest French restaurants in the city. Everyone at the table seemed to be in good spirits. We were enjoying the celebration with exquisite food and wine. Then I looked across the table at Savannah and saw that tears were falling down her cheeks. She stared at me with such pain in her eyes.

I will never forget that moment. I will never forget how my heart ached, but worse yet, how Savannah's heart was tearing apart.

I looked back at her, desperate to ease her pain. But I couldn't find any words. I thought, *what am I doing to myself? What am I doing to my kids?*

CHAPTER NINE

GETTING THE HELP
I DESPERATELY NEEDED

By day, I functioned reasonably well. But by sundown, my mind was obsessed with drinking. As each day came to a close, all my attention went to the bottle. My insides craved it. I needed to drink to pass out every night because I was in such a state of depression.

When I looked at my precious 16-year-old daughter during my birthday dinner and saw the tremendous hurt in her eyes, I hated myself for putting it there. The rest of the family appeared to not have noticed anything. But it was Savannah who had been living with my chaos.

Before that birthday dinner, she had confronted me about my drinking. She was right, of course, but I couldn't hear it. I didn't want to. It was too painful for me to look at my own self and the awful mess I'd gotten myself into.

Nobody mentioned anything during my birthday dinner, but the following weekend I received a phone call from my sister-in-law Ellen. She explained that she and Will were having a family cookout that Saturday afternoon. They invited me to come over. I agreed.

When I drove up the driveway, I knew something was up. By the number of cars outside, I saw that everyone was there. What was going on?

Will opened the front door and put his arm around me. He walked me down the silent hallway into the family room ...

There everyone was, standing in a semi-circle: Matt, my sisters-in-law Ellen and Kate, Savannah, Steven, Dad, and a pastor. It was an intervention. The tears streaming down the faces of Savannah and Steven are imbedded in my soul.

I paused for a moment and looked at these beautiful, familiar faces. They were filled with kind sympathy. No words were needed. A sense of relief went through my body. All I could think in my head was: *Thank you, God.*

Since I was a closet drinker, my family did not know the depth of my problem, at least not until Savannah brought it up to them. Dad said he had no idea. But how could he not have known? He was an addict himself. Was he too close to see the signs? Will and Matt had their suspicions, which were confirmed by their courageous niece. Ellen and Kate were unaware except for what Will and Matt had told them.

Of course my children knew. They lived with my addiction day in and day out. Steven had asked me to stop, but I couldn't. Savannah had talked to me about my drinking problem, but I didn't listen. Finally, out of her deep love and concern for me, Savannah sought help from my brothers. I am forever grateful to my daughter for saving my life.

The pastor, a recovering alcoholic himself, said with warmth in his eyes, "There's a spot waiting for you at the Betty Ford Center. Are you willing to go?"

Without batting an eyelash, I responded, "Absolutely."

Matt took me to my house to gather a few clothes. Then, off we went. It was that quick. The clinic was just a couple of hours away over the mountains and into the desert. As we drove, few words were spoken between us ... but what was there to say? Matt dropped me off at the front desk. As per the center's policies, he was not allowed to go any further.

My first stop was at the nurse's office. A physical was conducted to determine my condition. Luckily, I was not so far along in my addiction that my body had suffered. I was taken to my dormitory, which was for women only. The men had their own dorms. At my dorm I was met by a myriad of personalities—women who were angry and bitter, women who were detoxing from numerous drugs and alcohol, women who were reserved and aloof.

A wide range of ages, ethnic, and economic backgrounds were represented here, some on scholarship, others well off. Patients were doctors, lawyers, celebrities, businessmen, businesswomen, moms, dads, sons, and daughters. Any of them easily could have been the person next to you at work, the gym, church, or the PTA meeting. Addiction knows no boundaries.

I knew I didn't want to take another drink. I was intent on getting through this program and reclaiming my life. There was no looking back. For thirty days I took every aspect of the regimented program seriously: the chores, the meetings, the lectures, the group counseling, the one-on-one counseling. We woke up at six o'clock every morning. From the moment my feet touched the ground to bedtime, I had no free time whatsoever.

I knew the success rate for sobriety after getting help was low, but I was determined to never go back, never take another drink. For my thirty days of rehab I put everything I had into the program, though there were moments when I thought I did not have the strength to go on much longer. Deep in my soul I knew I had to press forward.

The clinic tried its best to make everyone's stay as comfortable as possible. Mrs. Ford was very hands-on. Warm and friendly, she would talk with all of us in the dining room. On one occasion, I just had to chuckle— she was wearing khakis and tennis shoes.

"The former First Lady wears tennis shoes, too!"

She was one of us. There was no segregation within these walls.

Six months after completing the program, I attended a dinner for alumni. President and Mrs. Ford were at the table next to mine. After the event, I wanted to be sure to thank them, so I went right up to President Ford, introduced myself, and told him how grateful I was for the Betty Ford Center. He smiled a kind smile. Then he looked directly into my eyes, placed his hand on my shoulder, and said, "I am proud of you. Keep up the good work."

There were no bodyguards keeping him at a distance. He was there to support his wife and all of us. I felt immense gratitude for the work the Fords were doing through this center. Their selflessness gave me and countless others a second chance at life.

A key phrase taught in recovery is "one day at a time." That's simply what life is anyway, isn't it? At the Betty Ford Center I spent time daily in the prayer and meditation room, a tiny but powerful space complete with a garden and gently running fountain. Alone in this room, I cried openly, wondering how all this had happened, how I'd gotten to this point.

I spent a lot of time thinking about Karine. I thought about her holding me, wrapping her arms around me and pulling me close in that special maternal way of hers. I had always felt safe in her arms. As I reflected daily inside this tranquil room, I invariably found my way back to Karine's sweet, familiar scent and simply lingered there a while, the world around me melting away. During these moments I felt a calming peace wash over me. Sometimes, I would quietly sing "Amazing Grace" to myself, a song I had often heard flowing out of Karine's lips while she bustled around the house. These memories provided the calm in the midst of my storms.

Other times, I would fall on my knees in humility and desperation crying out to God, "Help me!"

Buried somewhere in my mind was a glimmer of hope. I knew that the strengthening of my soul was a tangible possibility. It was not something that would happen overnight, but I knew that it would eventually come to be.

While sitting in that prayer room, I reflected on my teen years. Memories of singing at high school graduation drifted into my head. I recalled that culminating moment as my classmates and I walked down the nave of the cathedral in our long white ball gowns. It was a procession with more pomp than a Town and Country wedding—a procession symbolizing twelve years of the shaping and molding of proper Southern ladies, fit for society. I remembered walking into the alto section of the choir in the apse of the cathedral, feeling so ready and confident. Brimming with hope, we all sang together, voices in perfect harmony.

Gazing out over the sanctuary filled with parents, grandparents, siblings, and friends, I frantically searched for the one person I wanted to see. Then I saw her sitting in the back row, poised and with such dignity in her crisp white uniform, a big smile on her face.

Karine's eyes met mine. Tears filled my eyes as I beamed from ear to ear. My body relaxed, and I sang so joyously the words of the Lord's Prayer:

> *"Our Father, who art in Heaven,*
> *Hallowed be Thy name.*
> *Thy kingdom come, Thy will be done*
> *On Earth as it is in Heaven.*
> *Give us this day our daily bread,*
> *And forgive us our debts*
> *As we forgive our debtors.*
> *And lead us not into temptation,*
> *But deliver us from evil.*
> *For Thine is the kingdom, and the power, and the glory,*
> *Forever and ever, amen."*

We were so strong and hopeful, ready to face the future and make it our own. And now here I was, 25 years later, wondering: How did I get here? How did I stray so far that I ended up in this treatment center? Tears fell from my eyes, and I didn't bother to wipe them away. Their coolness against my cheeks provided some form of comfort as the memory of our voices singing that beautiful prayer came flooding back to me.

After I completed my thirty days, Will picked me up. I met him in the reception area. There was no fanfare or celebration, simply a smile and a hug. I could not expect my brother to understand the thirty days I had just experienced, and that was okay. I was just happy that he was there for me, there to support me on my journey.

Where was this journey taking me? Recovery certainly was not guaranteed, with a success rate that wasn't great. Before my thirty days had passed, tragedy struck—twice. A woman in my dorm left the center, went home, and drank herself to death. And an 18-year-old male drug addict who walked out those doors decided to take his life shortly thereafter.

Not long after I returned home, I learned of another tragedy. At the center I did chores—cleaning the kitchen and taking out the trash first thing in the morning— with a woman my age from Chicago. We hit it off from the start. She had such a contagious laugh, a fun personality. We were in therapy sessions together and sat at lectures together. She was scheduled to go home one day before me, and I remember watching her prepare to fly home. She was so excited to see her husband again and had dressed up nicely for him.

I was happy for her ... and concerned. Deep down inside, I wasn't sure she'd make it even off the plane without drinking. But I tried to shake that thought off. Once I got home, I called her to see how she was doing. Hearing her voice, I sensed she'd been drinking. A couple of weeks later I got a call from her husband. The sadness in his voice was evident when he said that she'd been admitted to another rehab center for a month. By the end of the summer, she had ended up in the hospital's psychiatric ward. I was so broken up over this.

I never heard from her again, and the last time I tried to reach her, the phone had been disconnected. I don't know what became of her.

To this day I ask, why? Why didn't they, why *couldn't* they, embrace a sober life? Why, why, why?

I will never know.

Will and I drove away from the center, away from what had been my home for the past month, a month that had felt like a lifetime. Across the mountains we traveled, leaving the desert behind. I did not look back. Few words passed between us, each of us lost in thought. This is how I re-entered my life.

Once I was back in the maze of the real world, I religiously applied everything the clinic had taught me. I saw a counselor without fail several times a week and attended AA meetings daily. Thankfully, not a cell in my body wanted to turn back to alcohol.

I did all my homework. If I needed to attend three AA meetings a day, I did. Every single day I thought, "I am not going to let this get me again. I am going to break the family chain of this insidious disease." There was no going back for me. I was determined to stay strong for me and for Savannah and Steven. I knew the disease was progressive. I'd seen it do its damage to people I loved.

Thank God, there is no desire in me to have another drink. But if the inclination ever does arise again, it will only take the sight of Steven standing in the street with tears in his eyes to stop me, or the image of Savannah crying in the restaurant that fateful spring evening. The memories of my son's tear-filled plea and my daughter's tear-streaked face still break my heart. So many years have passed, but I have not been able to go back to that restaurant.

I cannot emphasize enough how alcoholism destroys lives. It destroys entire families! The disease has taken so many people I love. I pray I am the last of the generations who has succumbed to this insidious disease. Though I can't control the next, I can be an example. I thank God every day for the gift of sobriety, for the strength that He has given me thus far.

And I know that looking down from Heaven, Karine is smiling at me and saying, "I'm so proud of you, my sweet Bethany Ann."

CHAPTER TEN

UNDERSTANDING DAD

Talking about Dad, the person who has had the greatest impact on my life, is complicated, if not impossible. How can I begin to portray the individual who on the one hand crippled me, but on the other hand provided for me and will always be my lifeline? In all the years I knew Dad, he never once uttered the words, "I love you," "I am proud of you," or "You are beautiful." All those endearing words any Daddy's little girl desperately wants and needs to hear never came forth from his mouth.

Not once.

I remember so clearly an incident from when I was ten years old. Mom had taken me to a salon. By then, my strawberry-blonde hair had turned dirty blonde and the soft curls were straight. Mom thought it would be best to perm my hair in order to recreate the natural curls I once had.

After the stylist got through with me, I looked in the mirror and was absolutely mortified. I couldn't help but burst into tears. My perm was unflattering, with my hair twisted abnormally—it looked nothing like the soft, natural curls I'd had as a little girl.

On the way home, I tried to keep the tears to myself, but they came streaming down my face anyway. Not only did I have short, chubby legs, but now I had a ridiculous hairstyle to go along with them! Mom shot me an angry look and said, "You better stop that. God is going to punish you for such complaining, and I am going to tell your Dad."

God punishing me was one thing, but being scolded by Dad was another issue altogether! I preferred taking my chances with God than facing the wrath of Dad.

Sure enough, he came home from work and Mom wasted no time explaining what had transpired. As I peered out my bedroom window, I saw my parents talking by the vegetable garden. Then Dad walked to the house with that deliberate stride of his, Mom by his side, and my heart started pounding. His lips sealed in a tight line, he ushered me to their bedroom and sat me down in Mom's chair. Facing him, my legs dangling a couple of inches off the ground, I braced myself for what he was about to say.

His eyes grew cold and dug deeply into mine. "Mom told me about what you said, and I don't approve of it," he spoke sternly. "You're being vain, and there's no use being vain, because you're never going to be pretty anyway, certainly not like your mom. So you have no business getting upset over a perm."

His lecture over, I was excused. The talk lasted less than a minute, but his words have never been forgotten.

Even though Dad said these sorts of things to me, I loved him always. He instilled in me character traits for which I am eternally grateful. Dad was a pillar of society. Through his regular example I learned valuable lessons in honesty, courage, tolerance, and respect. He taught me that all people are equal, no matter their walks of life, race, or color. I am deeply thankful for the values he gave me, but I would like to have had a different, more comfortable relationship with Dad.

All my life I felt I was never good enough in his eyes. Oh, how I desperately worked to get his approval! Good student, accomplished pianist, the coveted high school cheerleading position, editor of the high school yearbook, a pioneer female student at my college ...

It was not until the final days of his life, when I sat next to him on his bed in his home, that a breakthrough was made. Tears welling up in my eyes, I gazed upon Dad, a mere shadow of the giant of a man he once was. And I realized that he was simply another human being, like myself, who had done the best he knew how on this earth.

Dad was larger than life to me. I loved him. I feared him. He was a man with presence, a man who walked into any room and commanded attention. He was formidable in stature, both physically and mentally. At

6'2" he was quite tall, with shoulders so broad that when he sat in a regular chair, his frame towered over it and spread out like eagles' wings. I remember hiding behind those shoulders each time the wicked witch in "The Wizard of Oz" appeared on the television set! Her green, evil face would take up that entire screen, and I believed that if I hid behind Dad's shoulders, she wouldn't be able to see me.

Dad's long legs had a steady and deliberate stride. Since he moved so distinctly, I always knew when it was him walking down the long hallway in our house. His fair, freckled face, though boyish, was stern, with piercing hazel eyes that looked right through you. His voice was deep and commanding. Whenever he was angry and called my brothers and me by name, a shiver would jolt up our spines. Each time we heard that tone, the three of us knew that, more than likely, a belt or switch would be waiting to make contact with our flesh.

I remember how my whole body would tremble as the belt cracked against it. Fortunately, I never got the switch—probably because I was the baby sister—but Will and Matt did. I cringed whenever I saw my brothers get that switch. I would stand on the sidelines holding my stuffed bear, tears welling up in my eyes, crying, "No Dad, please!" But in those days, getting the switch or the belt was an ordinary way of disciplining a child—it was not looked upon as physical abuse.

In some ways Dad was a mystery to me. As a businessman he always was impeccably dressed, but when he relaxed at home he wore his favorite clothes until there wasn't much left of them. I still have his tattered navy blue terry bathrobe hanging in my bathroom. He wore it for years, and it shows. Dad was one to wear his favorite shoes until holes showed through. After he retired you never saw him in a tie. Here was a man who chartered the finest yachts, drank only the best vodka, but would complain about the rising price of movie theater tickets!

Strong-willed and determined, Dad didn't let much stop him. If he wanted to do something, he always found a way to do it, regardless of what the circumstances were. When smoking was banned on commercial flights, Dad said, "Damn it. I'll just buy my own jet." And he did.

Dad had a brilliant mind. Strike him up for conversation on any number of topics, and he could hold his own just fine. Math was a breeze for him. I remember how he'd get so frustrated with me whenever I asked for help with math homework. I'd sit on the arm of the chair in his and Mom's bedroom while he looked at the math problems and tried to explain the solutions. His brow furrowed, he spent hours trying to educate me on the language of numbers, yet I could comprehend none of it. Still, I pretended to listen closely. In reality I just wanted to sit next to him, to be close to him, to get him to cuddle with me and tell me everything would be okay despite my challenges with math. But those words and hugs never came. There were just even tones and the occasional eye contact, nothing more.

In addition to being a math whiz, Dad cooked the best homemade chili, which was always served with saltines and butter. This dish was a weekly Saturday night occurrence, and no one in the house ever grew tired of it. It was that good.

Despite Dad's striking presence and natural good looks, he wasn't perfect. I'd say God passed him by when handing out physical coordination—just like He passed me by when handing out long legs. Mom and I would laugh hysterically over Dad's unfortunate mishaps. One time, when I was 16, I walked out the front door only to encounter Dad dangling off a ladder propped against the house. The only thing keeping him from hitting the ground was a leg hooked through the ladder, and that leg was holding on for dear life.

At the exact moment I spotted Dad, Mom was driving up our driveway.

"Ted, what the heck are you doing?" she exclaimed, trying to hold back laughter.

Dad simply kept dangling, cussing away using all his favorite four-letter words. Mom and I practically rolled over with laughter, knowing full well that Dad had no business thinking he could master, or even attempt, any maintenance work.

On another occasion, Dad was lying on his sofa in his bedroom with a cup of coffee on his lap. Clumsily, he spilled the hot coffee all over himself and literally sprang out of his seat. Mom and I couldn't control our laughter, which only exacerbated his mood even further!

There was the time when he and I were walking through the vegetable garden; at one point he looked down, hands in his pockets, to find a water moccasin right next to his feet, staring up at him. He jumped in the air—to me it seemed like an entire six feet—and all his dollar bills went flying everywhere! Sweat dripping from his face, Dad took hold of a hoe and attempted to chop the creature's head off. He missed. Uninterested in Dad's antics, that snake just turned around and slithered away.

Years later came the ultimate blunder—the spreading of Mom's ashes.

Both Mom and Dad had expressed their wish to be cremated and have their ashes spread across a particular area of waters in the Exumas, a group of remote islands in the Bahamas. They loved those islands; we had taken numerous boating trips across the beautiful, clear, still waters there. In fact, Matt loved the islands so much he built a small house on one of them. Dad and us kids, daughters-in-law, and grandchildren went down to Matt's house in July of 1990 to release Mom's ashes. We powered out on his Boston Whaler to the most heavenly waters I had ever seen—the perfect combination of turquoise and azure. You could see the ocean floor and its abundant marine life. It was absolutely breathtaking.

Will gave a prayer, and all of us started sharing memories of Mom. Then it was time.

Dad opened the urn to spread her ashes. In typical style, he fumbled with the container. He ended up dropping the darn thing into the water!

"Damn it! Hell!" he cried out.

Matt quickly dove in to retrieve the urn. When he got back into the boat, he took over the responsibility of spreading Mom's ashes. I just looked up at the sky and giggled. I knew Mom was laughing and shaking her head, exclaiming, "My Lord, Ted!"

Dad lived ten years beyond Mom, but they were not quality years. A life of excessive drinking and smoking, along with a sedentary lifestyle, finally caught up with him. The summer of 2000, he began to fade quickly. He needed assistance to get around, so we hired a personal nurse. I spent weeks with him. Not only did I want to help out, I also simply wanted to be with him.

We had a good chuckle together one morning when I helped him take a shower. At this point, he was in a wheelchair. I wheeled him into the shower to bathe him.

"Who would have ever thought you would be bathing me!" he exclaimed.

During those last weeks I spent with him, somewhere in the back of my mind I was hoping to finally hear the words I had yearned for all my life.

He came very close to delivering them.

One morning I was massaging his shoulders when he said, "I can't believe you are being so nice to me."

"Why?"

"Because I have always been so mean to you."

Tears filled my eyes as I answered. "Dad, we have all done the best we know how here."

"Yes, but I am sorry for all the times I should have been there for you. And I expected too much."

"That's okay, Dad."

I simply continued to massage his shoulders. I knew this was Dad's way of telling me he loved me.

Will visited Dad daily. I left Dad's bedroom whenever my brother came by. I knew they needed privacy. From the hallway I could hear Will crying. I would peek into the bedroom and see him with his arm around Dad as he sobbed. I do not know what words were said. But I do know there'd been many years of pain between Dad and Will. I knew words of love and forgiveness were needed. Will needed closure, just as I had needed it.

Matt was away that final week. He had taken all the kids with him, to shelter them from what was going on. But when the inevitable came, he brought everyone home to see Dad before he passed.

Dad passed away the morning of July 7th. Will, Matt, and I were with him when he took his last breath. No words. Nothing left to say.

The mortician came to wrap Dad. It was the same kind black man who had wheeled Mom away ten years earlier. Once again he gently looked into my eyes with a knowing look. Once again I saw Karine's eyes, those soulful, warm eyes, filling me with comfort. Who was this man? Did Karine have something to do with bringing us together?

As he wrapped Dad, Will quietly said, "This is it." Seeing both Mom and Dad wrapped and wheeled away by a mortician without a doubt had a profound impact on my brothers and me, bringing us to see what's really important in life. We must truly love, truly forgive. Life slips away so very quickly. No measure of a privileged life can ever take the place of love and forgiveness.

Our family flew to those beautiful Bahamian waters to spread Dad's ashes in the very spot where we had spread Mom's a decade earlier. Back to those waters Mom and Dad loved so much. Once again, there was quiet sharing on the boat, but there was no drama this time. Dad wasn't there to fumble! I thought about that and giggled to myself.

CHAPTER ELEVEN

MY BROTHERS

Ever since I can remember, I've looked up to my brothers. They've served as my friends, protectors, and role models. Will is a man of honor, a man with an inner strength and a moral fiber rarely found in people. He was born in August of 1950, making him not quite four years older than me (I was born in April of 1954). But he always seemed so much older. He is one of those people who had the face and aura of an adult even as a small child. And since Dad was rarely around, I thought of Will more as a father figure than a big brother.

Though I cannot speak for him, in my eyes it always seemed that Mom expected him to be the responsible one, the one to take care of Matt and me. I don't think Will ever really had a childhood, or at least not the carefree childhood Matt and I enjoyed. He was quiet and serious, one who spent hours in his room reading and writing. Though I do remember one hilarious moment that took place outdoors ...

When Will was 12, he got a brand new bow and arrow set. The three of us siblings went to the woods to play with this new toy of his. Will wondered how far he could shoot an arrow into the sky. He pulled back that arrow with such determination and shot it so far in the sky it disappeared. We all thought it was gone, kind of like my parakeet.

But we were wrong.

Will bent over to pick up a rock and that darn arrow came speeding down from the sky, point first, and hit him directly in the butt. Thankfully it bounced off without piercing his skin, but it sure took all of us by surprise, Will especially as he jumped up thunderstruck.

There were Saturdays when my brothers and I would drive go-carts up and down our meandering driveway and street, pretending to be racecar drivers. During winter snows, we'd spend hours sledding down our street. I always felt special when Will played with me; I knew how much his books meant to him, so for him to take time out from reading to hang out with his little sister was a big deal.

When he got older, those years of reading and writing paid off. Will won the most coveted English literature award during his senior year away at a New Hampshire prep school. From there, he went on to Stanford.

At the time, I didn't understand why Will left home his high school junior year to attend school in another state. Mom and Dad explained that he felt his chances of being accepted into Stanford would be better from the New Hampshire school than from our local prep school. But I suspect he needed to leave home to be a teenager and leave his "oldest child responsibilities" behind.

I believe he left because he needed to find Will.

In the summer of 1969, when his freshman year at Stanford ended, Will revealed for the first time a vulnerable, compassionate side I'd never seen before. I will never forget that revelation. Upon his invitation, I had gone to Stanford for a visit at the end of his spring quarter. I felt so excited that my oldest brother had asked me to visit him at college! It was a big deal. Afterwards we drove back to Memphis together for summer break.

We started our long trek home in his Chevy sports car. With it being a multiday journey, we camped out in sleeping bags under the stars. Near Amarillo, Texas, I climbed into the backseat to take a nap (in those days, seatbelts were not mandatory). I'd been snoozing a little while when suddenly I woke up abruptly to a jolt.

One of the tires had blown out. In the blink of an eye, we swerved off the freeway into a pasture and headed dangerously toward a concrete ditch. I braced myself against the front seat, closed my eyes, and saw my life of 15 years pass before me. The next thing I remember was Will pulling me out of the backseat. He was in a complete state of shock as he gently lowered me onto the grass next to the freeway. The Chevy was totaled; it looked like an accordion.

A couple on the freeway saw the whole accident. They got out of their car and rushed over, then called for help from a nearby telephone booth. Returning to us, they spoke to me constantly to make sure I was conscious, and they stayed with us until the ambulance came.

The next thing I remember was lying in bed in the intensive care unit with tubes running up my nose and down into my stomach to check for internal injuries. Will, though unscathed, was delirious. He sat on my bed crying, holding me, wanting to be certain I was okay. I can still see the tears in his eyes and feel his arms wrapped securely around me. At that moment Will was no longer a father figure ...

He was my brother.

Matt was always the adorable one, Mom's favorite. Will and I knew it, but we were never jealous. That's just how it was. Who could resist Matt's smile, his charm? I certainly never could. And he knew how to charm Mom in such a way that she could never stay angry with him for long!

On my second birthday, Mom had set my birthday cake out on the driveway. She wanted to take a picture of me in my white, puff-sleeved smocked dress standing next to the cake and my new tricycle. Matt, in his cute shorts with suspenders and saddle oxfords, decided to go for a ride on my tricycle. Unintentionally, he ran directly over that beautiful cake. I looked down at the cake, then at him. He looked down at the cake, then at me. A smile spread across his face, and that was that.

Not quite two years older than me, Matt was my hero. I followed him around like a puppy. Whatever he did I wanted to do, from the days of playing Tarzan to going off to college. Growing up he played tennis and, therefore, so did I. He excelled at the sport, sometimes playing number one on the varsity team and even serving as captain. I also played on the varsity team, but I didn't excel like he did. Matt was editor-in-chief of his yearbook his senior year, so I worked hard on my school's yearbook and became editor-in-chief my senior year. He was a good student, and for him, it took very little effort. I was a good student, but for me, it took *a lot* of effort!

Matt was accepted into college in 1970. I visited him during the fall of his sophomore year. It was a beautiful New England autumn day, and I fell in love with the campus. The old red brick buildings covered in ivy captivated me. It was a world far removed from the South. He took me to a soccer game, which was played on a field surrounded by beautiful pine trees. I was instantly hooked and applied as soon as I returned to Memphis.

I spent two years at college with Matt before he graduated. He captained the guys' squash team and I traveled with the team to watch him play. We both loved art history, and we both majored in it. At that time it was a small department, so he and I often were in some of the same classes. I remember writing three blue books full for exams while he wrote only one, if that. Who always got the better grade? Matt did, of course.

He was always there for me when I thought the world was crumbling around me. Through my heart-aches and rough academic times, he was by my side. When Mom and Dad announced they were moving to Southern California, we both grappled with the fact that we would not be returning to Memphis.

As children we were inseparable, but as adults we each had to follow our own paths. The night of Paul's and my rehearsal dinner, Matt cried. Intuitively, he and I knew it was the end of an era and things would be different between us. They shouldn't have been, but they were. I started a new life as a wife and soon mother, while Matt remained single until his mid-thirties. I am pretty sure Mom had something to do with that; in her mind, no girl was good enough for him.

I know there were times when Matt needed me, but I was too busy with my own family. Ironically, Matt married Kate about the time my marriage to Paul began to unravel. Now I desperately needed him, but he was too busy with his new life. So I know we both have hurt each other, unintentionally. But both of us have forgiven each other in order to move forward. You just have to. Life is too short, too precious.

CHAPTER TWELVE

LOSING LOVED ONES

Though alcohol took many of my loved ones at young ages, a longevity thread does run through my family. Grandmother reached the age of 94, outliving her husband and three of her four children. Two of Grandfather's sisters, my aunts Ana and Eva, were centenarians, Eva living to 100 and Ana reaching the incredible age of 109. All three died simply of old age. Eva was in a nursing home and Ana, believe it or not, lived on her own until the age of 105, never missing a Cardinals game. After she turned 105, she moved in with a family. The two sisters lived in Missouri and had a good relationship, occasionally ribbing one another. Ana often accused Eva of being a hypochondriac because she lived in a nursing home!

Each year the sisters spent Christmas with Grandmother, and year after year the trio went on cruises together. I think Grandmother liked having a "one-up" on them—she always wore that mink stole of hers while they were in cashmere sweaters! I'm also pretty certain that Grandmother paid their way. Eva, who never married, was quiet, reserved, and tall like Grandfather, measuring 6' 1" in height. Ana was at the opposite end of the height spectrum, barely reaching 5'2". She was quite a character, a firecracker with lots of energy, never short of words. She married twice, outliving both her husbands as well as her son, whom she lost in WWII. Ana was an amazing woman; though she experienced a great deal of adversity, she never lost that zest for living. Her deep faith in God kept a smile on her face. Ana always wore a brown wig—the only time I saw her without it was when she was in her casket!

Savannah and I flew to Missouri for her funeral in 1999; Dad was too ill to go. I think the entire town of Independence was at Ana's memorial to honor her life. She was buried, as she had wished, next to her first husband and son. She never did like her second husband much.

Oh, how I wish I had asked Aunt Ana questions about her life! Here was a woman born in 1890 who died just one year short of 2000, a life fully lived until the end. She'd seen changes the rest of us only read about in history books. What a remarkable life my Aunt Ana must have led.

There is nothing more difficult than losing a loved one, someone who is close to us. I have experienced a great deal of loss in my life, and I've found it quite challenging to navigate away from the pain. Along with losing Mom and Dad, I have lost a number of amazing people who were near and dear to me.

Matt and I had a childhood friend named Amelia. She was the same age as Matt; both were born in 1952. She was an only child, and we knew her well because our dads were close friends. Amelia would play Tarzan with Matt and me, always taking on the role of Jane. By pulling together assorted rags from our house, she would concoct costumes for herself and Matt. Since I was Cheetah all I needed was a bathing suit. Decked out in our jungle attire, we went off to swing on vines across the creek in our woods for hours. Little did we know at the time that her life would be cut short.

Amelia had childhood diabetes. She was frail and fragile with porcelain white skin. An exquisite ballet dancer, she had such grace about her. Watching her, we all thought she would be on stage one day. She certainly had the talent, but life just didn't go that way for her.

Since her father was an officer in the military, she moved around numerous times with her parents. They lived all over the world. Through the years her diabetes progressed. The last time I saw Amelia was in August of 1990. Her parents had retired to Miami where they completely committed their lives to taking care of their daughter. The love between the three of them was so tangible.

Dad and I had stopped in Miami on our way to the Bahamas to spread Mom's ashes. Amelia was 38, and though diabetes had left her blind and crippled, she still had an amazing sense of humor and the most contagious laugh. She also had many vivid memories from our childhood. We sat reminiscing for hours before Dad and I left for the Bahamas. Soon after our visit, I found out that Amelia's mom had died of a heart attack.

In 1992 Amelia reached the age of 40, but her frail body succumbed to the illness, and she passed away. Her dad later said that after her mom's death, she simply lost the will to live. She wanted nothing more than for the two of them to be together, and God granted my friend that wish.

Sorrow crushed my heart after I learned of Amelia's death. I longed to see her again, to hear her marvelous laugh, to feel the warmth of her radiant smile. Why hadn't I kept in touch more often throughout the years? The finality of her death sat inside me like a block of lead. I missed her deeply.

Then there was my friend Billy.

Autumn was in the air that Friday night in September of 1972 when Patti and I, giddy college freshmen that we were, went to our first frat party at the "animal house." There he was, sitting on the stairwell, sporting the preppiest outfit I had ever seen. He had a huge smile, large hazel eyes, and wavy brown hair. When I got close enough, I caught a whiff of a sweet familiar scent. He was wearing Royall Lyme, the cologne Dad always wore.

As captain of the soccer team, captain of the squash team, and president of the Class of '73, he was certainly a popular guy on campus, what people affectionately called a BMOC—"big man on campus." I knew that he must have been a very confident guy as well, as he was brave enough to wear an I-Zod pink sweater and bright green corduroys!

He caught my eye and gave me a smile. "So you must be Matt's little sister."

Going into college, I knew I would be forever labeled as Matt's little sister, but I didn't mind.

A friendship instantly developed between Billy and me. Since I was a freshman and he was a senior, I felt he was too old for me to date, but I absolutely loved and adored Billy. Not only was he my friend, he was also a big brother to me. I often traveled with the squash team to watch him and my brother Matt play. I felt so proud being there, supporting two guys I dearly loved.

My friend Billy graduated in the spring of 1973 while I still had three years to go. Though I was sad that I would no longer see his beaming face around campus, life went on. For a number of years we kept in touch, updating one another on all the current happenings—marriage, kids...

He and his family moved around quite a bit with his job, and before I knew it, we had lost touch. Yet I never forgot Billy—that smile, that laugh, that confident ease he displayed. I would wonder at times: What if?

In November of 1994, while I was living in Memphis, the phone rang. It was Patti. Her voice was shaky. I immediately knew something was not right.

"Patti, what is it?" I asked.

"Billy has lung cancer," she replied, barely able to get the words out of her mouth.

My eyes welled up with tears, and my grip around the receiver loosened. Everything around me seemed to disappear. Billy? Lung cancer? How was this possible? He was the healthiest person I had ever known—athletic, never smoked, kept in great shape. How could this be?

He received a number of aggressive treatments over the next several months, but to no avail. Billy died in March of 1995, leaving his wife and three children. He was 45 years old. Patti and her husband Sam, who was Billy's best friend since our college days, flew from Rhode Island to North Carolina to attend the funeral.

I had made flight arrangements to go, but at the last minute, I decided I could not get on that plane. I just couldn't do it. I was paralyzed. How selfish of me. One of my dear friends had died—a dear friend with whom I'd lost touch over the years, a dear friend who never got to hear me say what he meant to me.

I never told him goodbye ... but he found a way to say bye to me.

A few months after Billy passed away, I found myself thinking about him, remembering the fun times we had together in college and feeling awful about not going to his funeral. That night I went to bed and soon fell asleep, but it wasn't long before I woke up and sat straight up in bed. Sitting at the foot of my bed with a big smile on his face, looking his dapper self in a tuxedo and smelling of the Royal Lyme cologne he always wore, was my friend Billy! I could not believe what I was seeing. After rubbing my eyes to get clarity, I was amazed to find him still there. Billy looked at me and kept smiling. He touched my leg, looked me in the eyes, and said, "Don't worry, I am very happy." Then, he disappeared.

Perhaps Heaven is closer than we realize ...

Losing a loved one is extremely difficult. When it's someone you think you are going to spend the rest of your life with, the emotional pain takes on a new level.

When I lost Ed, I felt as if the ground had been ripped out from underneath me.

Ed and I met in the fall of 2001. I had been asked to give an art history lecture to the docents at one of the fine art museums in Southern California where I was a member, and had at one time been a docent as well. While I was speaking to the group I noticed someone in the front row—a handsome, distinguished man with a headful of grey hair, bright blue eyes, and a nice smile.

There was something about this man.

He was looking at me and listening intently, not losing interest for a single moment. After the lecture, he came up to me. "That was great,'" he said, the most charming smile spreading across his lips.

"Thank you," I replied, smiling back.

"I'm Ed."

We shook hands and just looked at one another.

Outside, the rain pounded against the pavement. Preparing to rush to my car, I got my raincoat and umbrella and, in the process, dropped my books in the museum's foyer.

Without hesitation, Ed kneeled down and picked them up. After handing me my books, he helped me with my raincoat in a very gentlemanly way. I thanked him and headed out in the rain to the parking lot.

And that was that. Or so I thought.

Several weeks later, Ed called me at home to ask if he could audit the art history class I was teaching at a local university. He had obtained my number from an employee at the museum where we'd met.

"Of course you can," I responded. "It'd be great to have you in class."

We kept talking, and I learned quite a bit about Ed. He was ten years older than me and divorced. A retired Naval Commander, a fighter pilot in Vietnam. Twice he'd been deployed on the Kitty Hawk, flying a total of 262 combat missions over Vietnam.

In the spring of 2002 he audited my classes. That summer he invited me to lunch. We hit it off instantly. He was a passionate tennis fan like me; he was also a voracious reader and had a strong appetite for art history. We'd talk for hours on end about art. We started going out to plays and the symphony regularly.

It was just too good to be true. How did such a man come into my life?

Our romance was blooming into something very precious. By the spring of 2003 we were talking seriously about spending our lives together. He adored Savannah and Steven. And it was Ed who offered keen insight into Martin, now my son-in-law, before his first date with Savannah. Ed turned to me and said, "Those two are going to get married."

I looked at Ed quizzically and asked, "How could you possibly know this?"

Ed smiled. "I just know."

That summer, he and I rented a flat in London for a month. We attended numerous plays and chamber music concerts, hung out at museums, watched Wimbledon, and lounged around in Hyde Park. It was such a perfect time.

In mid-October, we took a road trip in Germany and Austria, flying to Copenhagen, a city I adore for its people, culture, the Northern Lights and long winters, for a couple of nights. I had spent a great deal of time there when I worked on my Master's thesis about a Danish artist, and I wanted Ed to take in the beautiful culture I had come to love. I was not teaching that fall so it was the ideal time for our adventure.

Winter was in the air. The mountains were dappled in snow. Fireplaces blazed every evening. I couldn't think of a more perfect setting.

One particular night in Salzburg during dinner, Ed suddenly grabbed his heart.

"What's wrong?" I asked, dropping my fork and reaching across the table.

He grabbed my hand and shook his head. "It's nothing—just a little spasm. I'm fine."

"Are you sure? Maybe I should call a doctor."

"Yes, if the spasms continue we will call a doctor. How's that?"

"Okay … but regardless, you should see someone when we get back home."

I was concerned, but I believed him. I thought that everything was fine, and I didn't want to overreact or bother him unnecessarily about seeing a doctor.

Throughout the entire two–week duration of our trip, he seemed to be in perfect health. We walked through Salzburg and Copenhagen, and I actually struggled to keep up with him. He was one of those people who could look at a city map one time and know the entire city by heart. Once that knowledge was in his head, he was able to walk confidently through foreign streets and feel right at home.

We went on a tour based on "The Sound of Music," visiting places in and around Salzburg where the film was made. I was beyond ecstatic about taking this tour. When the movie had come out in 1966, I was 12 years old and, falling in love with it immediately, I watched it a dozen times in the theater. Ed was 22 and already done with college when the musical made its debut. He was about to be sent to Vietnam as a fighter pilot, so he had other things on his mind. Needless to say, the movie didn't have the same impact on him as it had on me. Nevertheless, he was willing to take this tour— which was probably silly in his eyes—just for me, knowing it would make me happy.

Our last day in Europe was spent in Copenhagen in a renovated warehouse on the wharf where countless ships docked. It was a blistering cold, cloudy and windy morning. All of a sudden, Ed opened up the window and leaned out. With tremendous passion, he shouted as loud as he could, "I love this woman!" My proper Southern side was mortified at his impulsive act. My heart, however, leapt with joy.

When we returned to the U.S., it was a Sunday in early November. On Monday, we had lunch with Patti and Sam, who were visiting from Rhode Island. During that meal, Ed and I made plans to see each other on Wednesday. Ed was going to come to my house for dinner.

Wednesday came, and I didn't hear from him at all. There were no calls from him during the day, which was very unlike him. I called him, but there was no answer. I knew he had many errands to run that day, so I figured he was busy.

But when five o'clock came and went, and still there was no sign of Ed, I just knew something was terribly wrong. An uneasy feeling burning a hole in my stomach, I drove to his condo, which was twenty minutes away. As I pulled up to his place, I saw that his car was parked outside. The lights and TV were on inside.

I knocked on the front door and waited.

No answer.

I went around to the back patio and noticed the screen door was ajar. I shimmied myself over the stucco wall and walked in.

There he was, down the hallway, in his bedroom, lying on his back ... dead.

He was in his workout clothes, and his arms were angled behind his head, as if he'd been in the middle of doing a sit-up.

My breath caught in my throat.

"Oh, Ed! What did you do this for?"

Raw instinct took over. I grabbed the phone and dialed 9-1-1.

But as I dialed, I knew that there was no use. I knew he was gone.

I went through the motions of resuscitation and pumping his heart. He was ice cold. I knew he had been there since morning because that was when he typically worked out.

When the policeman arrived, he pronounced my beloved dead on the scene.

The first person I called was my brother Will.

"Will, Ed has died."

"What!"

"Yes. He's dead."

"I will be right there."

Within half an hour, Will and Sue Ellen arrived. We sat together in complete shock over what had transpired. Ed's suitcase from our trip was still unpacked— his London trench coat was hanging on a hook on his bedroom door. Very properly, Sue Ellen took the coat and covered his body.

Will was in as much shock as I was. Though they

had known each other only briefly, he loved Ed and considered him a good friend. He paced around the condo, looking at the collections of books. Material possessions weren't important to Ed, but his library was the West Coast version of the Library of Congress.

In the midst of looking around, Will froze when he saw a "To Do" list on the kitchen counter. At the very bottom of the list, Ed had written these words: "Call Doctor."

And do you know, the mortician who came for Ed was the same black man who had respectfully taken away Mom and Dad—that strong hulk of a man, wearing a black suit and black tie, with those kind, gentle eyes.

What were the odds of this? Who was this gentle giant? Could he be an angel sent by my dear Karine?

We exchanged a knowing look. No words were needed.

I called Patti, who had already returned to Rhode Island. The very next day she boarded a plane to Southern California to be with me. What a true friend she is. I've always thought of her as a "kindred spirit." She stayed by my side through everything — the wake, the memorial, the reception after the memorial.

In the hours, days, and months that followed, I struggled to heal.

Why hadn't I seen this coming? Why did God send me someone so perfect, only to yank him away in a blink of an eye?

The healing process was long and difficult, but I endured.

The summer of 2004 came, and with it a joyous occasion: Savannah and Martin married.

Ed had been right, after all.

I shared what he had said when I gave my toast, reflecting upon Savannah and Martin's first date. As I looked around the room, I saw knowing smiles and misty eyes.

Though our relationship was short-lived, I have no regrets. It was worth every moment—every conversation, every unspoken exchange communicated through our eyes, the laughter, the smiles, the joy, the enrichment. I would never trade places with anyone if it meant missing the opportunity to know Ed.

I think most of us fear death, regardless of our spiritual path, or we just don't want to acknowledge its inevitability. As for me, I am certain there is everlasting life with God. I know that I will one day reunite with my loved ones and even personages from centuries past. When? How? Will I live to see my grandchildren grow up and marry? Will I leave knowing that I did the best I could while on this terrestrial planet, that I learned the lessons I was supposed to learn? That I grew into the woman God meant for me to be? That when He sees me He will smile? So many questions. One day we will have our answers. Until then, all we can do is continue on our paths and love the people we are privileged to have in our lives. I do know that if Heaven does not have pearly gates, I will have to have a few words with Karine!

Before I knew him, Ed had had two heart attacks. Each time the paramedics rushed him to the hospital. And each time he stopped breathing en route. He told me that he remembered looking down on the paramedics pumping on his heart, and he felt a freedom that was inexplicable. "Death is the easiest thing you will ever do, Bethany Ann," he explained.

And, you know, after having seen death come to Mom and Dad and Ed—the peace on their faces, the quiet resolve—I believe he's right.

Ed had left me his copy of his favorite book, Henry David Thoreau's "Walden." Every year he read it on his birthday. For me, it symbolizes who he was. I had found it odd when Ed gave it to me. Did he know something was going to happen? Unbeknownst to me, he had one more gift to impart ...

One particular evening a few months after Ed had died, I was sitting on my sofa watching television. I heard shuffling coming directly from the loft above me. I turned around and looked up to find Ed standing there looking at me. His arms were crossed casually, and a big, content smile was on his face. He wore his Notre Dame sweatshirt and jeans, which he used to wear all the time. In a split second he was gone. But without a doubt, it was Ed. Yes, there is an afterlife. And Heaven is all around us.

CHAPTER THIRTEEN

TRAGEDY
AT THE MUSEUM

In the spring of 2004, a small fine arts museum that I was a member of—the same one where I had met Ed—arranged a members' trip to Italy. Though I wasn't one who typically went on group tours, something about this one piqued my interest. The itinerary was full of stops to enchanting towns: Rimini, Ravenna, Parma, Bologna, and Assisi. It seemed like a wonderful opportunity to experience firsthand some of the magnificent art I'd studied and lectured on but had never seen in person.

Ed had passed away several months earlier. It was time to move forward with my life. So off I went.

During the trip I got to know Jonathan, the museum's director, a little better. As a museum member and volunteer, I had known him socially for, I would guess, about twenty years. He was polite, full of conversation and laughter; but at times he was quiet, seemingly lost in his thoughts. There definitely was more to him than what he presented on the surface. There was a side that few, if any, ever got to know. During our Italy group trip, I got to see Jonathan as a devoted husband and dad who absolutely adored his wife and kids. He talked about them continually and was always on the lookout for the perfect pair of shoes for his wife.

He had a brilliant eye for art. Our museum was looking for a new acquisition; Jonathan invited me to a gallery in Milan to help him evaluate a few pieces. He had a natural instinct for which piece would enhance our already masterful collection.

To my surprise, after our trip Jonathan asked if I'd be interested in taking on the position of Education Coordinator. I was thrilled. I loved the museum's collection; it was an absolute jewel. And I thought the world of Jonathan. I felt truly honored to be asked to work there.

In January of 2005 I had my first day on the job. The staff was small and newly hired. All of us were excited to be there and ready to soar with fresh ideas. Among our many projects, one in particular stands out for me.

I had invited a string ensemble to perform the violin concerti "Four Seasons," one of the most popular pieces of Baroque music ever written, composed by Vivaldi, the seventeenth- and eighteenth-century Venetian virtuoso violinist. The performance was held in conjunction with an exhibition of paintings of the parable,

"The Prodigal Son," by the seventeenth-century Bolognese artist, Il Guercino. The juxtaposition of this moving, elaborate musical composition with the powerful, awe-inspiring paintings depicting Jesus Christ's most popular parable about forgiveness and mercy was surreal. One hundred people, from elementary school age to those in the winter of their lives, filled the foyer of this small jewel of a museum. When the music began, silence filled the room. Our senses of sight and sound were taken to higher, deeper levels. The paintings in all their drama and emotion were brought to life by this glorious, heavenly music. I was simply spellbound by this duality. It was one of those rare moments in life when one's physical and spiritual being are one.

Despite everyone's enthusiasm, I sensed uneasiness in Jonathan. I couldn't put my finger on it, but I wasn't the only person to notice that something wasn't quite right. In the two years that our small staff had worked together, we had observed Jonathan going downhill progressively. On any given week he went through various mood swings. Each morning, when we walked into work, we braced ourselves never knowing what kind of behavior to expect from him.

As the months went by, Jonathan retreated more and more into himself. There were days when I walked into his office and found him staring out his window, which overlooked the beautiful downtown skyline and the Pacific Ocean. But he wasn't enjoying the spectacular view; he was deep in thought, his face reflecting concern, sadness, maybe even something else. Once I went into his office to discuss something and he simply wasn't there. His body occupied his chair, but mentally he was far away.

"Jonathan?" I asked. "Is everything okay?"

"You know, Bethany Ann, sometimes I think how one day I would like to just drive off a bridge."

I froze. How does one respond to that? I took a deep breath. I looked warmly into his eyes, doing my utmost to reach him, to convey how valuable he was as a human being.

"Jonathan, you don't need to stay in this job if you're not happy. Just leave … take your family and move. Start over. Get some help."

Jonathan looked back at me, his forefinger nervously playing with his mustache, a look of despair overtaking his face. He had no more words.

There were members who put unnecessary demands on him. I saw them and heard them. Jonathan would cringe when certain ones walked into his office. I think he was just so stressed out by being yanked in too many different directions. And I always had the impression that he didn't feel qualified enough for his position. In addition he may have battled inner demons no one will ever know. It got to the point where he seemed to simply give up.

In December of 2006, the unthinkable happened. It was a Saturday morning. I had just gotten home from the gym when Jonathan called me.

How odd, I thought, Jonathan calling me on a Saturday morning.

His tone was kind, resolved. He thanked me for all I had done for the museum's education program. I was surprised. What had prompted Jonathan to call me at home over the weekend just to thank me? I was befuddled and, at the same time, I felt a sense of fear come over me without really knowing why.

The next day, I got my answer.

It came in a phone call from a member of the museum. Jonathan had committed suicide the night before. At the age of 57, he shot himself in the head, ending his life.

My knees literally crumbled beneath me. I sat down and wept.

Why? Why did he do this?

His wife! His children! His mom! His brother! A family that loved him so much and whom he loved so much.

I knew he was depressed—but not this!

Could I have done anything to help him?

My tears of sorrow turned to tears of anger, anger directed at the people whom he was always trying to please, yet never could. Anger at the unreasonable demands they had placed on him. People who had worked with him much longer than I had. Were they blind, heartless?

Poor Jonathan ... he had just given up on life, leaving so many questions unanswered. The three of us who'd been working in the office with him left the museum. We had to. For whatever reason, we'd been brought together at a moment in time that we will never forget, a horrible tragedy stamped indelibly in our minds and hearts.

Losing Ed was painful enough—and now this?

For a long time, I grappled with all kinds of explanations. I wanted to bring reason to this traumatic event. I wanted to imbue it with logic and insight and justification. I felt as if I owed Jonathan that much. He was good to me. I admired him. I gained valuable artistic insights from him. And then he was gone, just like that, by his own choice. All I could do was ask, "Why?"

Prior to Jonathan's death I had enrolled in a month-long art history class at the British Institute in Florence, Italy. Jonathan had encouraged me to go. I left in January of 2007, several weeks following his death. Something about that great Renaissance city was immensely healing. My soul was soothed by the hourly ringing of bells from campaniles, the quiet reverence of locals praying in the churches. It was winter, and the city was peacefully quiet.

Again and again, I found myself returning to the Brancacci Chapel at the Basilica of Santa Maria del Carmine. One of the frescoed panels in the chapel is an image by the great fifteenth-century Florentine master, Masaccio, called "Expulsion from Paradise." The anguish is achingly present in Adam and Eve's faces as the angel directs them out of the Garden of Eden. It is an anguish that is universal—something I believe all of us experience in our lifetime, encompassing regret, embarrassment, pain, and failure.

I was also drawn to San Miniato, that majestic Romanesque basilica atop the hill south of Florence, overlooking the city and its Tuscan surrounding. Late each afternoon the Benedictine monks chant in the crypt. Listening to them, an inexplicable peace filled me so completely. I was constantly reminded of how every man who entered that Order made his vow and did not leave that site for his entire life. Yet each face, young and old, was at peace. Filled with curiosity, I returned to the basilica often just to get a glimpse of those who might be tending the grounds or working in the gift shop. This was their life. Their devotion filled me with reverence.

Through my years of studying art history, I have become personal friends with some of the saints. When I think about Jonathan today I am constantly reminded what holy ground "his" museum is. Each painting is a masterpiece.

Jonathan would spend hours contemplating in front of Rembrandt's "St. Bartholomew," one of Christ's apostles believed to have been flayed alive. Everything about this painting is striking: the power of Rembrandt's brush, from the broad brush in Bartholomew's robe to the detailed brush in his rugged facial features; the drama created in the play of light and shadow on his face; that furrowed brow; those wise eyes gazing into the distance with a look of knowing. And then there is the knife in his hand, foreshadowing his ultimate demise. Simply put, his humanness.

I thought back to those instances when Jonathan stood there, seemingly spellbound by the images before him. What was going on in his mind during those times? What exactly led my dear friend to take his precious life?

Business continues. Exhibitions and cocktail receptions continue, as they should. In every arena, in every setting, in every city, town, and village around the world, life goes on after a tragedy. People go on, many wearing the masks they've worn their entire lives. Then there are those who can't wear the mask anymore. We may try, but sooner or later the mask comes off. No more small talk. No more jumping through hoops. No more trying to please others.

My guess is that Jonathan simply couldn't wear his mask any longer. And you know what?

Neither can I.

CHAPTER FOURTEEN

LIFE IS
A MIRACLE

Whenever I look at Savannah and Steven my heart fills with immeasurable joy. I am so grateful, so proud to witness the adults they've become. A loving wife and mom committed to her family, Savannah possesses an inner strength way beyond her years. Steven is now a young man embarking on the challenges of a career. In high school, his friends called him the "Universal Friend." He is like that even now, with his innocent, carefree attitude and acceptance of everyone; there is also a deep maturity that keeps him consistently centered and balanced.

As children grow up and pave their own roads, parents have to step back, let go, and release. But this can be so hard to do, can it not? Relationships change over time, and we can't fight that. It's simply part of life. As much as we want to hold on, we have to give in to the flow. We have to trust that the road ahead will open, promising to be a fruitful one.

As I look back, I recall the hours spent on my bed (our sacred spot) with Savannah and Steven, the conversations we had, the stories we shared, the laughter and the tears.

Even as a little girl, Savannah was mature beyond her years. At times it felt as though she was the mom and I was the child. When she was six years old and Steven was two, Paul and I took our children to Maui with his parents. We decided it would be fun to go parasailing. Savannah wanted to come along with us.

She and I went tandem. We started out confidently, hair blowing in the wind, our faces full of delight and enthusiasm. We were enjoying ourselves high above those beautiful Pacific Ocean waters when, suddenly and unexpectedly, we were dropped. Feeling helpless, I started to panic, worried we'd be dragged underwater. Sitting on my lap, Savannah looked up at me, held my hand, and said, "Mommy, it will be all right." And it was. We were soon up high again, as if nothing had happened. I'm still not sure why we were dropped halfway through our adventure, but my daughter got us through this unexpected turn.

So I shouldn't be surprised that when she was 16, Savannah stepped up to the plate to get help for me so I would stop drinking. Every day she saw what a grim impact alcohol was having on my life. She lived with a closet drinker and saw up close how I tried to hide my wine glass underneath my chair at night. She saw that I had lost interest in the parts of my life that I used to meet with joy.

Savannah was nine when my disease began and sixteen when I got sober. Not once did she neglect to show her love for me, even as my disease progressed. Steven was four years younger than his sister, but he also knew something wasn't right. He was always there for me. The three of us have a bond that I am forever grateful for, one that I would not trade for anything in the world.

One rainy evening, two years after I quit drinking, Savannah was driving her Honda, heading to her boyfriend's house. I was on my way to pick up Steven from the library, so I was driving down the narrow road behind her. Out of nowhere, a woman from the other direction did a 360-degree turn in the road and hit Savannah straight on. I saw the car accident from afar and immediately knew it was Savannah who was hit.

Mother's instinct kicked in. No panic this time. I sped to the site. Someone who had seen the accident had already called 9-1-1. When I reached the Honda I saw that the bag had inflated and Savannah was protected. She was obviously shaken up and bruised, but otherwise fine.

As I stood next to the car watching over Savannah until the paramedics came, both of us saw a man jogging towards us with a fire extinguisher in his hand. He put out the engine flames. When I went over to thank him, he had simply disappeared. Savannah and I looked at each other speechless. Yes, angels do walk this earth. And they appear in many guises. Memories of Karine flashed through my mind... how she protected me from those snakes whenever we went fishing... how she protected me from all the stares we would get on the bus... her talks about the pearly gates of Heaven... her holding Savannah in her arms as if she were her own child that last day I saw her. Could this have been...? Guess I will never know until I enter those pearly gates.

Savannah and I have rarely spoken to one another about the jogger, nor do we talk about that incident to others. We don't need to. It's one of those indescribable moments printed indelibly in our souls

The paramedics came, placed Savannah on the gurney, and took her to the emergency room. She was badly bruised and had an injured leg, but other than that, she was fine. That weekend she attended prom on crutches, with scars across her neck. But she was still radiant and gorgeous!

Today Savannah is happily married to Martin, relishing her roles of wife and mom of two young boys. My first grandson, Luke, was born in July of 2007, and my second grandson, Jacob, was born in February of 2009. I must confess, there is nothing like being "Nana". It's a joy I never could have imagined.

When we're brand new, young parents, we are so focused on the day-to-day, hour-by-hour, minute-by-minute concerns of learning how to take care of a baby that we overlook precious moments that come and go in an instant. But grandparents are given a free gift of living those moments fully.

Moments like the thrill of hearing the first cry when each grandson was born, seeing the joyful tears on Savannah's and Martin's faces, the grandbabies' first smiles, their first giggles, watching them discover their toes and play with their feet, those first wobbly steps, the first time they utter "uh-oh."

And the most tender and heartwarming moments for me—the first time each of them reached out their arms for me to hold them. So innocent, so trusting, so cuddly, so curious ... the circle of life continues.

Oh, to be able to bottle these moments!

When I look in my grandsons' eyes, the years are erased between us. To think, if I had not gotten sober I would not be "Nana" today. Come to think of it, if my life were not sober, there would be no life.

Hurt feelings can last a lifetime. Years can slip by with tension eating away at you, causing family gatherings to become strained and empty. Before you know it, years have lapsed and members have died. We realize how fragile, how short life is, often when it is too late. The core of family is so precious. It must be embraced.

We are given many chances. A day does not slip by without me telling Steven and Savannah, "I love you."

It doesn't matter whether it is in person, by phone, by e-mail, or by text. We cannot spoil our children with too much love, too much affirming touch, or too much genuine praise.

In life we're often living in the past or the future, forgetting the beauty of the present moment. In doing so, we let those precious moments slip by. As children we are busy craving to be adults. In our younger years, we're so focused on catching the perfect boyfriend or girlfriend, on getting the perfect grade to get into the perfect college. After that, it's on to the perfect graduate school, which will (hopefully) lead to the perfect job, the perfect husband, the perfect children … and if things don't quite work out, maybe even the "perfect" divorce, if there is such a thing.

The list goes on and on, doesn't it? All along the way, when we hit a particular milestone, we think we will forever be happy. But that's never the case. We never seem to be satisfied. We forget that life is all about wrapping our arms around each moment. That is all we have.

There are moments in my life that will never be forgotten, moments that I will forever treasure …

> *Karine picking me up, sitting me on the kitchen counter, and saying, "You know, sweet child, that Heaven has pearly gates!"*
>
> *The look on Matt's face when he rode his bike over my birthday cake.*
>
> *Will's face when that arrow just bounced off his butt.*

Catching lightning bugs.

Road trip with Mom, Dad, Will, and Matt in 1960 to California, along Route 66, listening to "Itsy Bitsy Teeny Weeny Yellow Polka Dot Bikini."

Catfish and hushpuppies at the Catfish Hotel.

The look on Karine's face when my parakeet vanished.

Dad's face when he saw that snake looking up at him.

Mom's bright smile as she listened to me talking about my dates.

AJ and that snazzy chauffeur's cap.

Patti befriending me as we sat on a bench that first week at college.

The first winter snowflakes in Maine.

The moment the doctor placed Savannah and Steven in my arms for the first time.

The first time Savannah and Steven wrapped their little fingers around my finger.

The look on Savannah's face, lunch box in hand, as she headed off to her first day of kindergarten.

Watching two strong doctors struggling to dislodge Steven' shoulders from my uterus.

The look of excitement on Savannah's face the first time she rode a pony.

Steven running around the bases of our makeshift baseball field in the backyard, a stainless steel bowl on his head, his diaper hanging down to his knees.

The moment Savannah looked into Martin's eyes and said "I do."

The moment I set eyes on Steven at LAX upon his return from a semester in Australia.

Listening from the other side of the delivery room, with Martin telling Savannah, "Push! Push!" And Savannah responding, "You try!"

The moments I first held Luke and Jacob.

Each time Savannah and Steven say, "Mom, I love you," before hanging up the phone.

Michelangelo's "Pieta" at the Vatican—the shaking of my knees, tears welling up in my eyes as I gazed upon Christ's lifeless body, completely surrendered, across His mother's lap.

The moment Sean and my eyes locked

Dancing around the May Pole to Tchaikovsky's "Waltz of the Flowers" on May Day my senior year of high school.

Sitting with Mom on her deathbed and looking at that little ten-year-old in the photograph—and Mom squeezing my hand.

Bathing Dad in his shower the week he passed away, both of us laughing awkwardly through it.

The scent of lilacs and dogwoods.

The ringing of the campanile bells in Florence.

The smell of raindrops.

Silence at the dinner table.

Matt hiding his okra in a milk box.

Canoeing on the White River and tipping over, with Matt stuck under the canoe, me feeling as if I'm drowning, and Dad surfacing and shouting, "Where is my fishing cap!!!"

Will holding me in the Intensive Care Unit.

My last weeks with Mom and Dad—the conversations, the forgiveness, the closure.

Being with Mom and Dad the moment each took their final breath.

Then there are the tangible memories left behind ...

Mom's simple gold and diamond pinky ring I always wear.

Dad's tattered navy blue terry bathrobe.

One of the last photos taken of Mom and Dad.

The Oriental art I grew up around.

The dolls Grandmother brought me from her many European adventures.

Gramma Ethel's hand-stitched quilt, well-worn and much loved, comforting one generation to the next—me at camp and college, Savannah at camp, and now serving as a blanket for Gramma Ethel's great-great-grandsons.

And of course, that precious photo of Karine and me standing in the kitchen— me in my white turtleneck and blue jumper, she in her starched, white uniform.

It is so important to tell the people in our lives how much we appreciate them. I think about Miss Maude, my friends Amelia and Billy, and particularly Karine. I never took the time to tell them how much they meant to me. I never even said goodbye. How I wish I had. However, that regret has instilled in me the will to never forget to show love and gratitude to those who are still here with us.

There's Mr. James, the one teacher who had the greatest impact on me, who is the reason I pursued art history. After 35 years I called him to say thank you. Let's never forget to thank all those people who have impacted our lives, if only for a moment.

Today, I am a mom, I am a grandma; I am a daughter and a sister, an aunt, a friend. I am a child of God. And my name is Bethany Ann. I was born Bethany Ann, and after six decades of life, I've decided to embrace the name I once thought did not suit me. Instead of looking to the future with expectations, I focus on the glorious present moment. At least, I *try* to.

For one never knows what life will bring, what lies around the bend. One road taken at a fork, one arbitrary decision made, can alter a person's life permanently. Some people seem to float through life with ease along a mostly straight, clear road, while others run into bumps and potholes no matter how hard they try.

Hearts of many are broken, sometimes irreparably. Hearts of others seem never to be broken at all. Many suffer the loss of loved ones early in life and innumerable times throughout the span of life, while others seem to go unscathed by such losses. And there are those who find it impossible to even live out their own lives. Some people suffer the cruel injustice of prejudices for a lifetime, whereas others are never aware of or simply never take notice of such injustice. Certain memories fade, while others remain.

Special people regularly come into our lives, some for just a season while others remain a lifetime. I thank all of them for leaving an indelible mark upon my soul. I do not have adequate words to completely express how fortunate I feel that God brought Karine into my life, a woman who simply loved me. Our relationship has lasted beyond a lifetime. Without this vital relationship, I can't even imagine how my life would have been.

It isn't just the ones close to us with whom we have a bond. All of us are alike in that each is a member of the human race traveling down a road in this life. And each of us has a story, a story that is shared by many whom we may never know.

THANKFUL
TO BE HERE

"Think of the good people who've left an enduring
mark on our character and our way of life. Many,
perhaps most of them, never offered a single word of
advice. But their goodness was so real that it spoke
for itself and drew us near, until we made it our
own. To this day, parts of many who are long dead
still live within us, not just in memory, but in the
very fabric and fiber of our soul."

— From *Finding Your Way in Troubled Times*
by Monsignor Dennis Clark

A gentle breeze hums through the air. The autumn evening is calm and cool. How long have I been reflecting on my life, on my uncommon friendship with Karine? The sounds of Steven, Savannah, Martin, Luke, and Jacob playing in the park bring me back to the here and now. I look toward them and watch them play for a moment before turning away and gazing back at the Pacific Ocean. Here, from this bench, I look at the golden-orange highlights in the sky. The sun has set, but the sky is still bright for a few moments longer. My entire body fills with warmth at the beauty before me. I surrender to the moment; I revel in it.

Hugging my legs to my chest, with my feet on the bench, I look out at the sparkling ocean. I feel its currents rocking inside of me. I feel its rhythms softly hypnotize, locking me into the present moment, locking me into the very core of the universe.

A black woman dressed in professional attire, probably in her early sixties, takes a seat next to me. After a long pause, she kindly comments, "Aren't the heavens beautiful this evening?"

"Yes, they are." Moments pass before I turn my head toward her and softly say, "You know, someone once told me that Heaven has pearly gates."

As I return my gaze back to the ocean she responds, "It surely does, my sweet Bethany Ann. It surely does."

Could it be?

But when I look once more, she is gone. Smiling to myself, I feel tears of joy and comfort forming in my eyes. I wipe them away.

Every life comes with a measure of brokenness from dreams unfulfilled, expectations unmet, hopes misplaced along the way. But this brokenness does not have to break us. We have a choice. We can either shut down, or we can open our heart.

I choose to smell the raindrops.

I look toward my family.

Steven and Martin are kicking a soccer ball to Luke and Jacob as Savannah, sitting on Gramma Ethel's quilt, looks on.

"Nana!" yells Luke and Jacob.

I direct my attention to my adorable grandsons, with their large, innocent eyes and beautiful smiles. Both are looking at me, waiting for me to watch them kick the ball.

"I'm coming!" I yell back.

My heart fills with irrepressible joy as I rise from the park bench and return to my family, my life.